By Gail Donovan

Other titles from Islandport Press

What the Wind Can Tell You by Sarah Marie A. Jette
The Door to January by Gillian French
The Sugar Mountain Snow Ball by Elizabeth Atkinson
Azalea, Unschooled by Liza Kleinman
Uncertain Glory by Lea Wait
The Five Stones Trilogy by G. A. Morgan

FINCHOSAURUS

By Gail Donovan

ISLANDPORT PRESS

ISLANDPORT PRESS

Islandport Press
PO Box 10
Yarmouth, Maine 04096
www.islandportpress.com
books@islandportpress.com

ISBN: 978-1-944762-65-0 (hardcover)
ISBN: 978-1-944762-55-1 (paperback)
ISBN: 978-1-944762-56-8 (ebook)
Library of Congress Control Number: 2018940792

Dean L. Lunt, Publisher
Cover, book design, and interior illustrations:
Teresa Lagrange, Islandport Press
Front and back cover art: Amy Preveza
Printed in the USA

For Gregory

Other middle grade titles by Gail Donovan

The Waffler
What's Bugging Bailey Blecker?
In Memory of Gorfman T. Frog

Table of Contents

Atticus Finch Martin

Deeper. If he could dig deeper, he could find something good. Not just a worm. He'd dug up plenty of worms. Not just a turd, which he'd also dug up, which he was pretty sure was the cat's, but who cared? He didn't want worms. And he didn't want turds. Unless it was a fossilized turd. Because that's what he wanted: a fossil. If a bulldozer driver like Edward McCarthy could uncover the fossilized tracks of a dinosaur only a few miles away, then he, Finch Martin, could find a piece of dinosaur, right?

"Thank you. Thank you," he said to an imaginary audience. "Thank you so much. I'm honored to have the dinosaur I discovered named after me—"

That was where Finch got stuck. Which name should he use? His first name was Atticus. His middle name was Finch. And his last name was Martin.

The Martin part came from his dad. The Atticus Finch part came from a book. His mom was so crazy for books that she a) was a librarian at his school, and b) actually

1

named him for a character in a book, which Finch thought was pretty weird until he got to kindergarten, where there were three kids named Atticus. So he started going by Finch, which he liked because a finch was a bird, and birds were related to dinosaurs.

But he still had to decide: *Atticusaurus? Finchosaurus?* Or *Martinosaurus?*

"The *Finchosaurus* was an amazing dinosaur—"

"*Finchosaurus?*"

That was Sam, his brother, interrupting Finch's famous-paleontologist speech.

"Maybe *Finchoraptor*," said Finch. "I haven't decided. It depends on what I find. Like if it's a plant-eater or a meat-eater."

Sam shook his head. He had carrot-orange hair, just like Finch. But orange hair was the only thing about them that was the same. Sam was a bookworm, like their mom. Finch didn't like books, unless they had plenty of pictures. And facts. Facts about dinosaurs.

"Mom says bedtime," said Sam.

"In a sec," he said.

Finch's brother was thirteen and in the eighth grade. At school, he and his friends roamed the playground like they were the biggest, baddest, meat-eating predators around. But even if Finch was just ten going on eleven, and in fifth grade, Sam wasn't the boss of him.

Besides, how could it be time for bed? The sky was still blue. The air was still warm and smelled sweet because he was digging underneath the lilac tree. Honeybees were still nuzzling the purple flowers. They weren't going to bed, and neither was he.

Sam loped off and Finch kept digging, shoveling up scoop after scoop of dirt. He stopped to watch their cat, Whoopie Pie, stalk a moth, her black tail switching back and forth, and then he went back to his digging.

"Finch. Time for bed."

That was his dad.

"I told you he was digging," said Sam, and made a told-you-so face at Finch.

"You must have been a woodchuck in another life," said Finch's dad.

"I'm not a woodchuck," said Finch. "I'm a paleontologist."

"Well, woodchuck or paleontologist, it's time to stop digging."

"Five more minutes," said Finch. "Please?"

"I like the *please*," said his dad. "But no. Besides, how can you even see what you're doing?"

Finch looked around. When had the sky gone from bright blue to inky blue?

"I can see," he insisted. "And this is for school. It's homework."

Technically, it wasn't a must-do homework assignment.

It was a choice. Tomorrow they were kicking off their new unit—'Digging Deep'—and Mrs. Adler had said anyone who wanted to could bring in something to share. And Finch wanted to!

Finch's dad crossed his arms over his chest. "Less arguing, Finch. More cooperation. Now."

Finch's dad was named Lester Martin. Everybody called him Les, which was a little funny because it sounded like *less*, which was pretty much what he was always telling Finch to do. Less bouncing (inside the house). Less digging (outside the house). Less asking why. Less arguing.

"But I need something for tomorrow! Why can't I stay up?"

"Bedtime," said Finch's dad.

It wasn't fair that Finch wasn't allowed to *not* answer a question from a grown-up, when grown-ups didn't answer his questions all the time. Or they just answered with a command. Stop digging. Go to bed.

"Come on, Finch," said his dad. "You too, Sam. Let's go."

"No way," said Sam. "I'm older—I'm not going to bed when he goes!"

"You're not that much older," argued Finch.

"Thirteen minus ten is three," said Sam, holding up three fingers. "Or can't you subtract?"

"I know how to subtract," said Finch. "But I'm practically eleven." His birthday was next month, in June.

Sam made a huffy, offended noise. "Yeah, and then it's my birthday and I'm fourteen. Plus, I'm in eighth and you're in fifth."

"So what?" asked Finch.

"Boys," said their dad. "Enough."

"What's going on out there?"

That was Finch's mom, coming across the grass.

"Wow," she said. "This is quite a picture."

Finch could picture it, too, just like in a book. Stars twinkling in the blue-black sky. Him digging underneath the lilac tree. And the caption would say: *On a warm spring night, a young Finch Martin dug up a fossil of the largest dinosaur ever to roam the earth, the* Finchosaurus.

But apparently Finch's mom saw a different picture.

"I see a kid up way past his bedtime."

"Mom, I need something for tomorrow," cried Finch. "Mrs. Adler said!"

"I'm sorry," said his mom. "But if Mrs. Adler has a consequence for you not getting your homework done, you'll have to pay it."

"Just one more shovel!"

"Now I see a kid who is digging himself into a whole lot of trouble," said his mom. "Because he is arguing with his parents. Les, would you give Finch a hand?"

Finch threw down his shovel and pawed through the dirt.

"I'm done!" he said. "I got it."

Finch held up what he had found. Wriggling around in the palm of his cupped hands, like it was just as unhappy about this as Finch, was a long, brown worm.

Maybe the worm was even more unhappy than he was, thought Finch the next morning.

He was just bummed because he had brought in a worm for sharing instead of a dinosaur fossil.

But the worm had gotten dug out of its home. Then, because nobody could find a see-through container with a lid, the worm had gotten put in a plastic bag of dirt. The bag was the kind with the zipper at the top, which Finch decided he'd better open, because what if the worm couldn't breathe?

He only unzipped the bag a little.

And he was only bouncing a little on his chair (which was actually a giant bouncy ball that Mrs. Davison, the occupational therapist, gave him because he had so much trouble sitting still on a regular chair).

But somehow he bounced the worm—and all the dirt—right out of the bag!

"Mrs. Adler," he called. "Mrs. Adler—I dropped my worm!"

Kids scrambled for a look, laughing and shouting and crowding in.

"Broccoli!" said Mrs. Adler.

Broccoli was Mrs. Adler's special code word. It meant everybody was supposed to stop doing whatever it was they were doing. Then back off. Step away.

Kids began backing away from Finch and the worm, while Mrs. Adler padded slowly across the room, like she was a *Giganotosaurus* and the kids were just some *Microceratops*, too small to worry about.

Mrs. Adler was actually pretty tall. She wasn't *old*-old, like some of the teachers, with gray hair. She was just regular grown-up old, with brown hair she wore clipped up into a messy bun.

Mrs. Adler looked down at Finch. She looked at the worm. She looked at the dirt spread all over the floor. She shook her head, as if she had known all along the bouncy ball was a bad idea, and now she had proof. Then she told Finch that she would call the janitor to clean up the dirt, and that he should go outside and put the worm in the class garden. She asked Grammy Mary, their class volunteer, to go with him.

Five minutes later, Finch was outside. All by himself. Well, by himself, with Grammy Mary. The playground was empty because nobody was at recess. The sky was an empty, no-cloud blue.

He didn't want to leave the worm on top of the ground, so he set down the bag and started digging. Then he saw something white in the brown dirt. What was it?

A tiny piece of paper. Not a scrap, but a big piece, folded and folded until it was as small as his thumb. Finch unfolded and unfolded, until it was flat, and he could read what was written on it. A single word.

Help.

Digging Deep

Finch dropped the worm into the empty hole and stuffed the paper in his pocket, feeling something already in there— ooh, jelly beans!—and went over to where Grammy Mary was sitting on a big boulder.

Perched on the rock, Grammy Mary reminded Finch of a gnome. Her hair was white and she was almost the shape of the boulder—short and round. She was wearing a purple shirt that said *I brake for unicorns*.

Grammy Mary came every day to help out in Mrs. Adler's room. Finch wasn't sure exactly how she was supposed to be helping. She didn't try to teach anybody anything, because she wasn't a teacher or a teacher's aide. Sometimes she walked with kids going to the nurse's office or for special services. Sometimes she sat with kids in the hallway if Mrs. Adler said they could take five minutes to "collect themselves." But mostly her job seemed to be saying hello. And smiling. *Hello!* she said to each kid as they arrived. *I'm so glad to see you!*

She gave him her usual big smile now.

"All done?" she asked.

"Yup," said Finch, nodding and holding out his hand. "Jelly bean?"

Two jelly beans—one purple and one green—sat in the palm of his hand, which even he had to admit was pretty dirty. Most grown-ups would say no thanks.

Grammy Mary picked the purple one. "Did you find a new home for that little guy?"

Finch popped the green jelly bean in his mouth. "Yup," he said.

Because that was the truth. He had found a new home for the worm. He didn't tell Grammy Mary about what else he had found, though. The note that said *Help*. Because he didn't want any help with the help note. He was going to find out himself: Who had written it? What kind of help did they need? And why had they buried it? Maybe they had hidden it there like a wish—like when you put a baby tooth under your pillow and hoped to get something good in exchange.

Back in the classroom, Finch dropped onto his bouncy chair and checked the whiteboard for the date. Because that's what real scientists did. They kept track of their discoveries.

Date: May 21

Place: Acorn Comprehensive School, Oakford, Connecticut

Object found: a scrap of paper with the word Help

"Welcome back, Finch," said Mrs. Adler. "Take out a few pieces of paper, and write each letter of your name on a different one. Who can tell Finch why we're doing this?"

Mrs. Adler and Finch both looked up and down the rows. She was wondering who to call on, and Finch was wondering who needed help. There was a chance it wasn't somebody in this room, but Finch doubted it. Each classroom had its own garden plot, and you weren't allowed in another plot. Probably it was one of the seventeen kids in Mrs. Adler's fifth-grade class. Sixteen, not counting him.

Right now, half the class had their hands raised in the air. Graciela (who loved to answer questions). Oscar and Oliver (who loved to hear themselves talk). Charlotte and Halcy and Millie and Khalid and Mohamed.

The other half kept their hands down. Angelika and Fatouma and Samantha and Quinn. David and Kael and Noah and the Atticus who went by Atticus.

"Oscar," said Mrs. Adler. "Why are we writing the letters of our name?"

Oscar answered, "Just because?" and looked at Oliver for approval. Oliver cracked up, laughing.

Mrs. Adler took the not-dignifying-this-with-a-response approach, and moved right along. Graciela was waving her hand back and forth, holding a pencil with a fluffy, puffy thing on the end. Usually Mrs. Adler tried to keep things fair, which meant not always calling on Graciela. But probably she wanted to get the right answer this time.

"Graciela?"

"Poetry."

"Poetry. Yes," said Mrs. Adler. "But who remembers the kind of poem we're going to write?"

"Oliver!" shouted out Oliver without being called on.

"Oscar!" shouted Oscar.

Mrs. Adler didn't say anything to Oscar and Oliver but she wrote their names on the corner of the whiteboard, right under the word *Warning*, and Grammy Mary pulled her chair up right beside Oliver. Then Mrs. Adler looked around, searching for a kid who had actually been listening ten minutes ago.

"Angelika?" she called.

This was the first year he and Angelika Sanchez were in the same class, and she didn't talk much, so Finch didn't know much about her. But if Mrs. Adler was calling on her, it meant she thought Angelika probably knew the answer. Angelika didn't answer, though. She just shook her head and twirled her long, dark hair around her finger.

Nobody had their hands up anymore. Mrs. Adler took a chance on Noah.

"Noah?"

Noah Smith-Dodson was the kind of kid who knew the answers but hardly ever raised his hand, because he wasn't a show-off. Finch knew plenty about Noah, because Noah was his best friend. He had two last names—one from each of his parents. He had two dogs, too— a poodle at his mom's house and a chocolate doodle at his dad's. And the coolest thing about him was kind of gross: He had webbed toes. On each of his feet, the two littlest toes were stuck together.

"Acrostic," answered Noah.

"Correct," said Mrs. Adler, finally smiling a smile as big as one of Grammy Mary's. "You are going to write an acrostic poem. Each letter of your name will begin a word that describes you. But I don't want you to pick the first thing you think of. That's why you're starting with a whole page for each letter, with lots of room for lots of ideas. Now is the time to really dig deep to answer the question: Who are you?"

Finch almost rolled off his bouncy-ball chair. *Dig deep*?

"Mrs. Adler!" cried Finch, not waiting to be called on. "Mrs. Adler, when are we starting the new unit?"

"This is the new unit, Finch."

"I thought it was Earth Science!"

Mrs. Adler closed her eyes for a second and then opened them, as if she was hoping that this was a dream and when she woke up, he would be gone.

"Is that why you brought an earthworm to school?"

Finch nodded. Yes.

Mrs. Adler shook her head. No.

"No, Finch," she said. "I didn't say anything about Earth

Science, and if you had been listening, you would have known that. 'Digging Deep' is a poetry unit. Now please settle down and get to work."

Finch picked up a pencil and wrote down the first letter of his name. F.

Not being able to settle down was the whole reason Finch had started digging in the first place. His mom used to say, "Finch, you're bouncing off the walls. Settle down with a book, or go outside."

Reading a book or going outside? That was a no-brainer. Finch always chose outside. Outside, he didn't feel quite so bouncy. But he still had to do something. So he had started digging. Whenever he was digging, it felt like he could "settle down" and be doing something at the same time.

And there were so many cool things under the ground. Some were alive, like clams (he dug those up from the mudflats when they visited his grandparents), and worms and beetles. Some had been alive a long time ago, like bones and fossils. Either way, everything under the ground was like a wrapped present at a birthday party. And he was going to unwrap it.

"How are you doing, Finch?" asked Mrs. Adler.

"Good," said Finch.

To show how good he was doing, he wrote the other letters of his name, one to a page, in big capital letters. I. N. C. H.

H, for *Help*.

Finch had a good feeling about this. A pile-full-of-wrapped-birthday-presents feeling. Somebody needed help, and he wasn't going to stop digging until he found out who.

If You Had Thought of That

"That's so funny," said Noah. "Did you really think 'Digging Deep' was gonna be a science unit?"

Noah thought most things were funny, which was one of the best things about having him for a best friend.

"Yeah, thanks for telling me," said Finch. "Did you know it was gonna be poetry?"

"I did," said Noah, and in his best Mrs. Adler imitation, added, "and if you had been listening . . ."

Finch laughed. "Come on," he said. "Green Team!"

"Green Team," echoed Noah. "Let's go!"

It was the lunch/recess block, but after lunch Finch and Noah hadn't gone to recess. As members of the Green Team, they got to go up and down the halls every Monday, checking the recycling bins in all the classrooms.

Up until last year, "all the classrooms" had meant kindergarten through fifth grade. That was when Finch's school was called Acorn Primary. Then the town decided to change everything. Instead of having four elementary schools and two middle schools, they were going to have four schools that went from kindergarten through eighth grade. Finch's school turned into Acorn Comprehensive.

So the year Finch got to fifth grade—the year he should have been king of the school—all of a sudden there were kids who should have been in middle school, roaming the halls and the playground. Big kids. When he and his friends should have been the big kids!

At least none of the big kids was on Green Team. They didn't think it was cool. That was one of the good things about Green Team. Also, he got to wear a Green Team badge that meant he could roam the halls. Also, he got to visit all his old teachers.

"Hi, Mrs. Murphy," said Finch, bouncing into his old kindergarten room.

"Finch and Noah!" said Mrs. Murphy. She was by herself, eating a sandwich. A sign on her desk said *Warning: Peanut Butter in Use.* "You two are peanut-friendly, right?"

They nodded, and she pointed to the big green bin. "All right, then, do your stuff."

Finch took his time rummaging through the recycling bin. He loved being back in his old room.

He loved the chairs that looked so tiny now. He loved the terrarium where they kept a toad in the spring. He loved it when Mrs. Murphy used to play music so everybody could "dance their wiggly-jigglies out." She hadn't minded that he was so bouncy. She hadn't minded that he couldn't use scissors, or make the L-sound. Kindergarten had been the best.

But by first grade they had him so busy trying to fix all the things wrong with him that he was out of the classroom—away from his friends—more than he was in it. He had speech therapy with Mrs. Hunter. He had occupational therapy with Mrs. Davison. And he sometimes had to go see Mrs. Blake, the social worker, to talk about how he should be a cooperator with Mrs. Hunter and Mrs. Davison.

"Plenty of recycling," whispered Noah, "and no yucky garbage. Let's give them ten points."

"Wait," said Finch. "Let's look for extra points."

The classroom with the most recycling earned the Golden Bucket Award for the week. Mrs. Murphy's class hadn't won yet, and Finch wanted them to. He kept searching, turning over pieces of paper. Because a class could get *Every piece of paper has two sides* bonus points for paper written on the front and the back.

Noah kept track, counting aloud. "One, two, three, four, five, six . . . seven!"

On the clipboard, Finch wrote 10 + 7 = 17.

Then he cried, "The Green Team strikes again!" zooming from the room and zigzagging down the hallway, with Noah right behind him.

The hallway of this wing was extra good for zigzag

zooming because it was so wide. It was extra wide because K–1 kids didn't have hallway lockers; instead, they had cubbies in their rooms.

Lockers.

Finch stopped short. Noah, right behind him, stopped short, too—by crashing into him.

"Hey!" said Noah.

Lockers. Lockers were where he could look for clues. He shoved the Green Team clipboard at Noah.

"Take over, will you?"

"By myself?" asked Noah. "Why? What's up?"

A little part of Finch wanted to tell Noah. He and Noah could investigate together, like Green Team. But a bigger part of him didn't want to tell. He wanted to do this himself.

"Nothing," he said. "I just gotta go somewhere."

"Where?" demanded Noah.

"Nowhere," said Finch. "I just . . . gotta go."

"Oh," said Noah, with an I-get-it grin. "Like, you gotta *go*?"

Finch didn't have to *go*—not the way Noah meant—but he said yes anyway.

"Yeah, I gotta go. Like, bad. You do the next room and I'll catch up, okay?"

A minute later, Finch was standing by the fifth-grade lockers. There were two fifth-grade classes—Mrs. Adler's and Mrs. Tomlinson's. Finch knew the note couldn't have been buried by a kid from Mrs. T's class, though, because they had their own garden plot.

He made a field note in his mind.

May 21. Lunch/recess block. I began investigating an area close to where the note had been found.

But he didn't begin investigating right away. For one thing, even though lockers didn't actually have locks, looking in anybody else's was against the rules. For another thing, he couldn't decide which one to open. He scanned the row of lemon-yellow lockers. Some had magnets stuck on the outside, so kids could find their locker quickly. Finch's had a magnet of a *Stegosaurus*. Noah's had a foot. People were always giving him toy feet as a joke, because of his toes. There was a magnet of an angel. He wondered if that was Angelika's locker.

Which made him wonder—how come she hadn't raised her hand, even though she probably knew the answer?— when he heard somebody coming. He froze.

"Finch! *Hello!*"

It was Mrs. Hunter, the speech therapist. Finch used to see a lot of her back in first and second grade, when he was tromping down to her tiny office once a week to learn how to make the L-sound. And the R-sound. And the S-sound.

"How have you *been*?" she gushed. She always gave some words an extra zing, like she was sprinkling hot sauce on them. "I *miss* you!"

"I'm on Green Team!" he blurted, pointing to his badge.

"I'm allowed to be here!"

"Well, don't let me stop you," she said, giving him a funny smile. "*Carry on.* And make sure you drop by and say hello sometime!"

Finch waited until she was out of sight. Then he waited until his heart stopped feeling like it was punching him from the inside. Then it was time. He took a breath. Reached out to the locker in front of him. Silver handle—up. Yellow door—open. Inside—

"Hey!" came a voice right behind him.

Finch turned around to see . . . Angelika! Looking fierce. *Tyrannosaurus rex* fierce. Like she could rip his arm off, if she decided to.

"What are you doing in my locker?" she demanded.

Finch had two options. Tell the truth—that he was looking for clues because somebody needed help. Or not.

He picked *not.* It wasn't exactly *picking,* though. It wasn't as if he had time to think, *Should I tell the truth, or tell a lie?* It was more like, *If you're in a fight with a* T. rex, *you're just gonna defend yourself!*

"I'm not in your locker!" he said.

"You totally are," said Angelika. "It's my locker, and you're in it!"

"I made a mistake," tried Finch. "I thought it was mine."

Angelika shook her head. "No way," she said, pointing down the row of lockers. "Since yours is way down there.

Why were you looking at my stuff?"

"I *wasn't* looking at your stuff!"

Which was true, technically. Sort of. He had opened the door, but he hadn't touched anything. He hadn't even had a chance to look at anything!

"Yes, you were!" she shouted, pushing him aside and slamming the door shut.

"Was not!" he shouted right back.

Which was when the door to their classroom opened and *Giganotosaurus* stepped into the hall. Otherwise known as Mrs. Adler.

"Finch Martin," she said. "Angelika Sanchez. What's going on here? Why aren't you two where you're supposed to be?"

"He was looking in my locker!" cried Angelika.

"I was not!"

"Was, too!"

"Broccoli!" said Mrs. Adler.

Finch backed away. So did Angelika.

"Three breaths," commanded Mrs. Adler, staring at Finch as if he might not breathe if she wasn't watching.

Finch took three deep breaths. So did Angelika.

"Finch, come with me," said Mrs. Adler, "and Angelika, please go back to the playground for the rest of recess."

Angelika started to run off, then caught herself. Running in the halls wasn't allowed. She speed-walked away.

"That's not fair!" blurted Finch. "How come I'm in trouble and she's not?"

But Finch already knew why. Some kids could do almost anything and teachers still assumed they were innocent. Angelika was one of those kids. So even when Mrs. Adler didn't know what had happened, she took Angelika's word for it. She figured Finch was the troublemaker, because he was always bouncing around and because this morning he had bounced a bagful of dirt all over the classroom.

Since they both knew the answer already, Mrs. Adler didn't bother answering his question. Instead she asked, "Is there anything you want to tell me?"

For a second, Finch thought about showing her the note. What if she knew he had a good reason? He'd still be in trouble, but *maybe* not as much. But for sure he'd lose the note. He'd lose the secret. He'd lose the investigation.

Finch shook his head. No. Nothing to tell.

"All right, then." Mrs. Adler turned and began striding down the hall. "Follow me."

Finch tagged along beside her.

"I have Green Team!" he tried. "Noah's waiting for me."

"If you had thought of that," said Mrs. Adler, "then you wouldn't be here now."

Finch decided Mrs. Adler shouldn't be *Giganotosaurus* anymore. She should be a whole new species: *Iffosaurus.* The dinosaur that could destroy your day with the word *if.*

If you had been listening, you would have known the new unit was poetry, instead of something good.

If you had thought of that, you'd still be having fun with Noah, instead of being marched down to wherever she was marching him.

Awesomeraptor

Waiting was not something Finch was good at. Luckily, he had the bench in the school office to himself. He started at one end and slid on his butt until he reached the other end. Then he went back to the first end. Then back to the other end.

"Finch," said Mrs. Stuckey, the school secretary.

"Sorry," said Finch.

He sat still for a minute, trying to decide whether it was worse to wait for something you wanted to happen—like dessert. Or something you didn't want to happen—like a friendly chat with Mrs. Blake, the social worker.

Then he started sliding slowly along the bench. He would slide so slowly that Mrs. Stuckey wouldn't even notice. Because he didn't want to make her mad. She was the one who gave passes to kids who were late. She kept track of the attendance sheets. Basically, she ran the whole school. After five years here—six, counting kindergarten—Finch knew enough to try and stay on Mrs. Stuckey's good side. And that's why he was moving . . . in . . . slow . . . motion.

"Finch!" said Mrs. Stuckey.

"Sorry!" said Finch.

"Let's put that energy to good use," she said. "Come lend a hand."

Mrs. Stuckey explained the job. She had printed 150 pieces of paper, each with two copies of the same notice. She needed each page cut in half, so she could send 300 notices home with 300 kids.

"Like this," she said, showing him how to use a ruler to tear each piece in half.

"Hey, you should get some Green Team points!" said Finch. "You're saving paper!"

"I'll settle for some help," she said, laughing.

Finch took the first piece of paper, but before he tore it in half, he read it. *Attention Parents: Due to the number of snow days this winter, it is necessary to extend the school year. The last day of school is now Tuesday, June 19. Please mark your calendars!*

"My birthday!" said Finch, right out loud. "Mrs. Stuckey, the last day of school is my birthday!"

"That's great," said Mrs. Stuckey.

"It's not like I want the year to be longer," said Finch. "But if it's gonna be longer, at least it's going until my birthday. 'Cause that never happened before! I never, ever got to hand out birthday cupcakes. And you never got to wish me Happy Birthday on the announcements. This is gonna be the first time!"

"Well, that's something I'll look forward to," said Mrs. Stuckey, giving him a big smile and taking the stack of papers.

"But I didn't finish," he said. "I didn't even start!"

"You can help another time," she said, pointing to the open door of the social worker's office. "Mr. White is ready for you."

"Mr. White?" asked Finch. "What happened to Mrs. Blake?"

"She's home with her new baby," said Mrs. Stuckey. "Mr. White is filling in. And he's waiting for you."

Finch dropped his speed into slow motion again. He walked. Slowly. Into the social worker's office. He took a seat. He looked around.

Same old office, with kids' artwork plastering the walls.

Brand-new social worker, Mr. White.

Mr. White matched his name—white skin and snow-white hair and beard. But the rest of him was definitely *not* white. He wore a bright red-and-white-checked shirt that reminded Finch of a tablecloth.

"So," said Mr. White. "Atticus. How are you?"

"Finch," corrected Finch.

"Sorry," said Mr. White. He glanced at a thick folder on his desk and read aloud, "Atticus Finch Martin. So, you go by your middle name?"

"Because there are so many Atticuses," said Finch.

"Got it," said Mr. White. "Awesome. Thanks for letting me know. I'm still getting up to speed here. So, Finch," he tried again. "How are you?"

"Pretty good," said Finch, jiggling in his chair.

"Awesome," said Mr. White.

Finch nodded in agreement. This guy sure liked the word "awesome."

"So, are you looking forward to summer?"

Finch could never understand why grown-ups asked that question. It almost seemed like they were pretending to be stupid. Because there was no such thing as a kid who *wasn't* looking forward to summer vacation. Or maybe it was some kind of trick question? Finch couldn't figure it out. Finally, he just told the truth.

"Yep," he said.

"Me, too," said Mr. White. "Summer is awesome. What do you like to do during the summer?"

Now Finch knew what was happening. He had been expecting a lecture about personal space and private property. But *Awesomeraptor* wasn't rushing straight toward his prey. He was trying to sneak around and ambush him. He was trying to get Finch talking until Finch told him why he was looking in somebody else's locker. No way!

"Umm," said Finch, "just . . . stuff?"

"Like, what kind of stuff?" asked Mr. White.

Finch shrugged.

"I might go camping with my dad," he said. "And my mom always takes me and my brother to Maine to see our grandparents."

"Awesome!" said Mr. White.

"Awesome," agreed Finch, nodding.

Except he had just remembered something that wasn't awesome.

Every summer they went to visit Gammy and Guppy. (His grandma had been Grammy until Finch couldn't make the R-sound, and then she became Gammy. Finch couldn't remember how Grandpa had turned into Guppy.) His grandparents lived on the coast of Maine. That's where Finch dug clams from the mud. Gammy soaked the clams in water to get the sand out, and steamed them, and they ate them dipped in butter.

But Finch had forgotten something. Gammy was in a nursing home now. Guppy was still in their house, but Finch's mom kept saying things like, "We'll see how long he can manage." Finch figured that they would still go visit his grandparents. But it would be different.

"Finch?" asked Mr. White. "Something on your mind?"

"No," said Finch. "Not really."

Mr. White kept asking friendly questions and Finch kept giving friendly answers until finally, the bell rang.

31

"Well," said Mr. White, "I better let you go. But it's been great getting to know you. Let's talk again soon, okay?"

"Sure," agreed Finch, "that'd be awesome."

He bolted from the social worker's office. He had gotten away! He had escaped from *Awesomeraptor*!

But not from his mother.

When he got back to his classroom, Mrs. Adler handed him a note. Finch wondered what it would be like to *not* have your mom working in your school, finding out everything instantly.

Hi Finch! Please wait for me after school, so we can walk home together. I'll come find you on the playground. Love you! Mom.

Finch would rather have walked home with Noah, as usual. But instead, when the last bell rang at the end of the day, he had to wait for his mom. And waiting was still not something he was good at.

The afterschool sky was still an empty, no-cloud blue, but the playground wasn't empty, like it had been that morning. It was full of kids in aftercare, swinging on the swings, scaling the spiderweb climber, swarming over the field in a soccer game. Finch didn't feel like swinging, or scaling, or swarming.

He felt like looking for more clues.

May 21. I excavated the area on all sides of the original find. I excavated about five holes. Each hole was about five inches deep. There was nothing in the holes, so I excavated five more holes, for a total of ten—

"Finch!"

Finch looked up.

His mom was standing there, with a look on her face that meant she did not see a scientific dig. She saw ten piles of dirt beside ten unauthorized holes.

Worse, she wasn't alone. On one side of her stood *Iffosaurus*. On the other, *Awesomeraptor*.

Mr. White had a look on his face that said, I think I need a few more friendly chats with this kid.

Mrs. Adler had a large piece of paper in her hand.

24/7, My Friend

"The paper said *what?*" asked his father at the supper table.

"Help," said his mom.

They weren't talking about *his* paper. The tiny piece of paper he had dug up from the garden. Nobody had seen that one. And now it was folded back up to the size of his thumb and squished inside a small tin box that used to hold Band-Aids. Under the table, he stuck his hand in his pocket. Touched the box, double-checking. Safe.

That wasn't the paper his mom was talking about. She was talking about a different piece of paper. Poetry paper. Which Finch did not want to discuss. He wondered if he could steer the conversation in another direction, like when a cop directed traffic, blowing a whistle and waving his arms around to say, *Don't go this way—go that way!*

"Can I have the pasta?" he asked. "I'm starving!"

"They're writing acrostic poems," explained his mom. "Each letter of his name will be the first letter of a word."

She scooped a spoonful of tortellini onto her plate and

passed the bowl to Finch's dad, who served himself and passed the bowl to Sam.

"We did those in fifth grade, too," said Sam, as he dumped a huge spoonful of tortellini onto his plate.

Finch was thinking about those picture books where you searched for what was funny, or wrong, in the illustration. What was wrong with this picture?

Not the hair. All the Martins had orange hair. His and Sam's was bright orange, like it was straight from a bottle of tempera paint. Apparently, their mom and dad used to have that bright orange color, but now their hair looked like some white had been mixed in. But, basically, their hair was all the same.

What was wrong with this picture was the food. Everybody had food except him.

"Food, please," he said. "I'm hungry, here."

"*Stargazer*," began Sam. "*Appreciative. Mellow.*"

"Stargazer?" scoffed Finch. "You don't stargaze!"

"Mrs. Adler said it could be a metaphor," explained Sam, as he took another giant spoonful, then launched into another list. "*Marvelous—*"

"Wait!" interrupted Finch. "We have to do last names, too?"

"Whoa, whoa, whoa," said their father. "We are getting way off track. Let's get back to the *Help*."

Sam didn't get back on the track their dad wanted. He

stayed on the Sam track.

"It was optional," he said. "Like, if you had a short name, you could do your last name, too." Waving the spoon, he recited, "*Marvelous, Artistic, Risk-taker, Toast-lover*—which was sort of silly, but she let me do it—*Inventive, Nice!*"

Sometimes it felt like Sam wanted to hog everything. Like the pasta—and Finch was hungry! And all the attention—which tonight maybe wasn't a bad thing. But it was still annoying.

"You're not a risk-taker," objected Finch. "You're a tortellini-taker. Mom, he's hogging it. I don't have *any* food."

"I love your poem, Sam," said their mom. "Now please pass your brother the pasta."

Finally! Finch got the tortellini from the bowl to his plate, to his fork, and into his mouth. Yum. Soft and salty, with cheese.

His mom kept going with the report to his dad.

"Mrs. Adler was concerned because Finch had written out all the letters of his name, like he was supposed to, but—"

"One letter on every sheet," interrupted Sam. "First draft!"

"Yes, thanks, Sam, I get the concept," said their father. "Now let your mother talk."

"But the only page he had worked on was the letter H. And the only word he had written was the word *Help*. All over the page."

"Finch?" asked his dad. "What's this all about?"

Finch shrugged and tried to say, "I don't know," but his mouth was full of food, so it came out more like *Hm-mm-mo.*

"Maybe he needs help writing the poem," suggested Sam.

"But that's not everything," said Finch's mom. "Mrs. Adler found him going through other kids' lockers."

"*Stealing?*" asked his dad.

"*Hm-mm-ma!*" said Finch. He swallowed and tried again. "I did not! I didn't steal anything! I swear!"

"Let me get this straight," said his dad. "You wrote *Help*, not once, but many times. Then you—at the very least— went into somebody else's locker."

"I didn't take anything!" said Finch again.

Which was true, so he tried to put an I'm-telling-the-truth look on his face. Then he put more tortellini in his mouth. Yum.

"That's not the end of it," said his mom.

"There's more?" asked his dad.

"After school I found him digging in the school garden."

"News flash!" said Sam. "Finch Martin dug a hole!"

"Not just one hole," said Finch's mom. "A lot of holes." She turned to Finch. "Honey, what's going on with you?"

Finch tried to figure out a good answer. The only thing "going on with him" was that he was on a mission. A mission to find out who had buried a note that said *Help*. And it was a solo mission. He wanted to do it by himself, without any help from anyone. Which meant not telling his mom what was going on.

He took another bite, for that special sound effect—talking with your mouth full. "*Nuffeeng*," he said.

"Please swallow, and answer me, Finch!"

Finch swallowed. "Nothing," he said with a shrug.

"Finch, if you say you weren't stealing, I believe you," said his dad. "But it still doesn't sound like nothing's going on."

"It sounds more like something," agreed his mom.

"He just wants attention," complained Sam. "Don't give it to him!"

"I think that's exactly what we're going to do," said his mom. "We're going to give Finch lots of love."

That was another reason Finch didn't like long books with lots of words. Some of them were books on how to be good parents. Like the one his mom and dad had read about what to do when kids were in trouble. Give lots of love. And pay lots of attention.

Finch speared a tortellini and popped it in his mouth, wondering how he was supposed to do *his* investigation, when they were going to be investigating *him*? Because "lots of love" in Martin-mom-and-dad speak meant one thing. He was under surveillance.

"Lots and lots of love," agreed Finch's dad. "Like, twenty-four/seven, my friend."

Double Blackmail

Just like she always did, Grammy Mary chirped, "Good morning, Finch!" when he walked into the classroom the next morning.

And Finch said, "Hey, Grammy Mary," just like he always did.

Then he made his way over to his desk and plopped down on his bouncy ball, just like usual, and other kids drifted in and took their seats. Just like usual.

Everyone was acting like everything was the same as always. Except he knew it wasn't. Finch started swooshing back and forth, because how was he supposed to sit still until he found out who needed help? He was still swooshing when the bell rang for morning announcements, and Mrs. Stuckey's voice came on over the loudspeaker.

"Good morning, boys and girls. Welcome to Acorn Comprehensive. Today is Tuesday, May twenty-second. Hot lunch today will be breakfast for lunch."

"Yes!" shouted Oliver.

"Yes!" echoed Oscar.

Mrs. Adler held a finger to her lips: Shhh.

"Today we are wishing Happy Birthday to Liam Woodbury."

Birthday wishes!

Finch felt like his insides were bouncing around. And that made him feel like he needed to bounce on the outside, too. He started back-and-forth swooshing, and up-and-down bouncing, all at the same time. He was swoosh-bouncing. He was bounce-swooshing. Because this was the year he was going to hear his name over the loudspeaker. This was the year he was going to bring cupcakes to class.

"Last, but not least, this week's Golden Bucket winner is Mrs. Murphy's kindergarten class."

Yes!

Mrs. Stuckey was wrapping it up. *"We have one more month of school, so there is still time for your class to win. Keep up the good work on recycling, and have a wonderful day!"*

The door opened and the Atticus who went by the name of Atticus came in, late.

This was his first year at Acorn, and Mrs. Adler had never put them together when she split them up into small groups. So pretty much all Finch knew about Atticus Paley was what he could see: shaggy, sandy hair on his head, and sneakers with no socks on his feet. In between, skinny.

"Good morning, Atticus!" said Grammy Mary.

Atticus didn't answer. He just walked to the back of the

room to hand Mrs. Adler his late pass, dropped into his seat, and turned his face to the window.

Now Finch knew who he wanted to investigate first. Atticus.

Except how was he supposed to do that, the way the desks were arranged now?

For most of the year the desks had been bunched in pods of four, so you could at least talk to the kids in your pod. But after spring break Mrs. Adler had split the pods up into rows. She said that rising sixth graders needed to be doing a lot less talking and a lot more working.

She had also moved her desk to the back of the room—*behind* all the student desks—so she could watch them when they were supposed to be working.

Which meant that Finch wasn't going to be able to talk to Atticus until lunch.

At lunch, the cafetorium smelled like scrambled eggs and French toast, and sounded like a hundred and fifty kids talking at the same time.

Finch went through the lunch line with his tray and then stopped in the middle of the room. If everything was still normal, like last year, he would have looked for Atticus around the best tables, by the windows. Those tables should have been for kids in Mrs. Adler's or Mrs. Tomlinson's class. Fifth graders.

But Acorn Comprehensive had "Learning Leaders," which was something about big kids showing little kids how to behave. Which meant they didn't give the middle-school-aged kids their own lunch block. First lunch was 150 kids from K through 8, and so was second lunch. Which meant the eighth graders had taken over the best tables.

Finch was still scoping the room, but before he found Atticus, Noah found him.

"Hey!" called Noah, waving. "I saved you a seat!"

Finch plunked his tray down on the long, picnic-style table and slid onto the bench seat opposite Noah, because there was no way you couldn't sit with your best friend at lunch. They both opened their milk cartons, stuck in their straws, and slurped some milk.

"I hate these healthy lunches," complained Noah. "No more chocolate milk."

"No more potato chips," agreed Finch.

"What am I supposed to do with this?" asked Noah, holding up an apple slice. "Put it in my ear?" He held an apple slice to each ear. He had just gotten a buzz cut, so his ears already seemed to stick out from his face. Now he had giant sticking-out apple ears.

Finch cracked up. "I can't hear you!" he said, laughing and holding an apple slice to each of his ears, too.

"That's because you weren't *listening*," said Noah.

In unison, they said, *"If you had been listening . . ."*

Finch was still laughing when somebody set their tray on the table and sat down beside him.

"What's up?" asked Sam.

"Nothing," said Finch, on his guard.

Sam always sat with his eighth-grade friends at lunch. The only time he had sat with Finch was when they were forced to because it was Siblings Day.

"What are you doing here?"

Sam peeled the tinfoil off a plastic cup and poured big swirly circles of syrup over his French toast.

"Here's the deal," he said. "Mom and Dad want me to spy on you."

Noah asked, "They *said* that?"

"Obviously, no," said Sam, spearing a French toast stick. "They said it would be nice if I could be a good big brother during the day."

"And you said *yes?*" asked Noah.

"They said they'd make it worth my while," Sam explained.

"Like, *pay* you?" asked Noah.

"They didn't say that, exactly," admitted Sam. "They just said they would really appreciate it. *Wink wink.*"

Finch groaned. "I don't believe this," he said.

"So here's the deal," said Sam. He ate another French toast stick and licked the spork. Making them wait. "Why

45

don't you show me how much you'd appreciate me *not* being a good big brother?"

"How am I supposed to do that?" demanded Finch.

"Duh," said Sam. "Money. You give me your allowance and I'll tell Mom and Dad that we eat lunch together every day."

"That's blackmail!" said Noah.

"It's a deal," said Finch.

"Shake on it, little brother," said Sam, holding out his French-toasty spork.

Finch took hold of the sticky spork and shook on it. Then Sam let go, leaving it in Finch's hand.

"You've got yourself a deal," he said. "And I'm outta here." He picked up his tray and headed for one of the eighth-grade tables.

"Wow," said Noah. "I'm glad I don't have a big brother."

"You're lucky," agreed Finch.

Noah really was pretty lucky, thought Finch. He didn't have any brothers or sisters trying to hog all the attention at home. Or blackmailing him. Plus, he got to have *two* dogs—Penny the poodle at his mom's house and Rozzy the chocolate doodle at his dad's. Finch couldn't think of any reason Noah would have to bury a note that said *Help*.

"So, what gives?" asked Noah.

"What?"

"Yesterday you ditch me during Green Team, and now your parents are on your case."

"So?"

"So, spill," said Noah. "Or I go tell your mom about the blackmail."

"But *that's* blackmail!" objected Finch.

"It's, like, double blackmail," agreed Noah, grinning and giving him a whaddya-gonna-do shrug.

What *was* he going to do? Yesterday he hadn't told Noah. And then he hadn't told Mrs. Adler, or Mr. White, or his parents. But now that all the grown-ups were on his case, maybe he could use a little backup. Besides, Noah was his best friend. If he was going to tell anyone, it would be Noah.

Noah put an apple slice to his ear again. "I can't *hear* you," he said in a singsong teacher voice.

Finch grinned, and gave in.

"Okay, fine," he said. "But you have to promise not to tell *anybody*."

Do Not Disturb

Noah wasn't the one who ended up telling; Finch was.

Because he had no choice.

An hour after lunch he and Noah and the rest of Mrs. Adler's class trooped into the library, which smelled like cooked eggs because it was right down the hall from the cafetorium.

"Welcome, everyone," said his mom, handing out rulers. "Welcome. I want to remind everyone to please use your mark-the-spot rulers when you take a book from the stacks, so you can put it back in the *exact right place* if you decide you don't want it."

Filing past his mom, Finch took a ruler. "Thanks, Mrs. Martin!" he said, as if he was just a regular kid.

"You're welcome, Mr. Martin," said his mom. "Happy book hunting!"

Kids fanned out across the room. Everybody was supposed to choose two books—one of poetry and one for free-choice. Finch cruised by the poetry section and grabbed

Bone Poems, which he happened to know was poems all about dinosaurs. He picked *Dinosaur Valley* from nonfiction, another old favorite. Then he took one of the "traffic signs" his mom had made and hurried to the end of the stacks, with Noah right behind him. They plunked down on the carpet behind the sign: *Do Not Disturb: Student Reading.*

"Let's make a list," whispered Finch.

"And split it," agreed Noah. "So, write everyone down."

They both knew all the names of the kids in their class by heart, alphabetically. Finch started writing, beginning with the first name: Angelika.

And then there she was, right out of nowhere, just like last time!

"What are you guys doing?" she demanded.

"Nothing," said Finch.

"Nothing," agreed Noah.

Angelika knelt down beside them. "It doesn't look like nothing," she said, pointing to the list. "It looks like my name!"

How did he get here again? Him against *T. rex*, with the same two options: Get into another fight—and that hadn't gone so well the last time—or tell the truth. But before he could make up his mind, things got worse. What was worse than a showdown with a *T. rex*?

Momosaurus!

"How's everybody doing?" asked his mom. "Did you

find something to read?"

"*Bone Poems*," said Finch, "and *Dinosaur Valley*."

His mom frowned. "How many times have you read those books?"

Finch grinned. "About a hundred?"

"I knew that," she said. "How about you, Noah? What are you reading?"

Noah looked at the book in his hand and said the title as if he was seeing it for the first time. "*For Laughing Out Loud: Poems to Tickle Your Funny Bone*," he said. "That sounds good!"

"You sound surprised," said Finch's mom.

"No—I mean, this is a really good book, Mrs. Martin. You really should read it."

"Thank you for the suggestion, Noah. Maybe you'd be willing to write up a *Who Loves This Book? Noah Does!* recommendation?"

"Definitely," said Noah. "Absolutely."

"Excellent," said Finch's mom. "How about you, Angelika? What did you find?"

"I found a book on birds," she told Finch's mom. "It looks really good."

"Great!" said Finch's mom, with a big smile for Angelika and an I'm-not-done-with-you-yet look for Finch.

Now that Acorn Elementary had become Acorn Comprehensive, Finch was going to have to wait until high school before he didn't see his mom at school every day. But what if his mom switched jobs and went to the high school when he did? What if she followed him around for the rest of his life?

"Thanks," said Finch, when his mom had moved on.

"You owe me," said Angelika. "Big-time."

"I know," admitted Finch, trying to think of what he could trade with Angelika so they'd be even. "I could put your name in for a Sunshine," he suggested.

A Sunshine was an award you got for "spreading sunshine." Any student who was nominated got their picture pasted to a yellow construction-paper sun and taped to the wall in the front lobby, around the giant construction-paper oak tree that was supposed to represent Acorn Comprehensive.

Hugging her knees to her chest, Angelika rocked back and forth. Thinking about it. She wore lime-green Crocs on her feet and a lime-green scrunchie at the end of her dark brown braid.

"No, thanks," she said. "I'm already on there for holding the door for some kindergartners."

"How about candy?" asked Noah.

Angelika pointed to her braces. "Not allowed."

Finch sighed. "What, then?"

"You tell me what you guys were talking about," she said. "And I won't tell your mom you were writing down *my* name, on the day after you went into *my* locker."

Yesterday, the *Help* note had been *his* secret. All his.

By lunchtime today he had told Noah, but that was cool. You could have a secret with your best friend.

But now, was he going to have to tell Angelika, too?

He thought about the story of Sue Hendrickson, the day she found a fossil in South Dakota. For a while, she had worked by herself, scratching the soil and brushing it away. Hoping this was something big. All by herself. And that must have felt amazing.

But when her dig-mates came back from town, she got to show them. She got to let them in on it. And then they were in it together, unearthing what turned out to be one of the best, biggest, most complete *T. rex* fossils ever found. *Tyrannosaurus Sue.* And that must have felt . . . *Tyrannosaurus*-amazing.

Finch pulled the tiny Band-Aid tin from his pocket. He took out the scrap of paper and unfolded it, showing the single word: *Help.*

"I'm trying to find out who wrote this," he said.

"*Help*," said Angelika, reading the note aloud. "Wow. Where'd you find that?"

"In our class garden," he said. "Buried."

"So why were you looking in *my* locker?" she pressed. "Did you think *I* wrote it?"

"No," said Finch. "I mean—I don't know. It was a little

random. I was standing there and I saw your angel magnet, and I wondered how come you don't raise your hand, even when you know the answer?"

"Hello?" interrupted Noah. "I don't raise my hand when I know the answer."

"Yeah, but I know you," said Finch. "I don't know Angelika."

Angelika's lime-green Crocs rose and fell as she rocked back and forth again. "It's because I'm busy," she finally said.

"Busy doing what?"

"I kind of . . . make up stories. In my head. I know I can half-listen and still get the assignment."

Noah summed it up. "You mean you're spacing out?"

"*You're* spacing out," she said, grinning. "*I'm* using my imagination."

Noah grinned, too. "So, you're not going to tell his mom, right?"

"Right."

"Thanks," said Finch. "You really should get a Sunshine!"

"Except you can't nominate me because you'd have to say what for, and this is secret," she said. "Right? Nobody else knows?"

"Yep," agreed Finch. "Just us three. So, what do we think? Who was it?"

Broccoli!

Angelika, Atticus, Charlotte, David, Fatouma, Finch, Graciela, Haley, Kael, Khalid, Millie, Mohamed, Noah, Oliver, Oscar, Quinn, and Samantha.

Those were the kids in their class, and that's how they wrote down their names. Alphabetically, including themselves, because that's the way they knew it by heart.

"It could be Atticus," said Finch. "Something's up with him. He came in late today and looked really bummed."

"What about David?" asked Noah. "He gets shaken down for milk money every day by Oscar and Oliver."

"For real?" asked Angelika. "How come?"

Noah shrugged. "They think it's funny."

"That is so not funny," said Angelika.

"Not cool," agreed Finch.

"What about Charlotte and Haley?" asked Angelika. "They both got head lice, and Charlotte's mom thinks Haley gave them to Charlotte, and Haley's mom thinks Charlotte gave them to Haley. So now their moms won't let them go over to each other's houses after school."

"Wow," said Finch. "How'd you know that?"

"Look," said Angelika, pointing to where Charlotte and Haley were sitting together, reading, their heads wrapped in blue bandannas.

"Bandannas!" said Finch. "Angelika, that was smart!"

"Thanks," said Angelika.

"All right, people," said Noah, in his best Mrs. Adler imitation. "Let's focus! It's gross to have lice on your head, right?"

Finch and Angelika nodded. Yes. Gross.

"And not being allowed to hang out with your best friend stinks, right?"

Finch and Angelika nodded. Yes. Stinky.

"But are either of those reasons enough to make you write a note for help?"

"Sure!" said Angelika.

"So which one of them wrote it?" asked Noah. "Charlotte or Haley?"

"Maybe they did it together," said Finch. "Since they're best friends."

"Maybe," said Noah.

"How come you're acting like it couldn't be them?" demanded Angelika. "'Cause you don't want me to be the one who figures it out?"

"Whoa," said Finch. "Come on, you guys."

Noah and Angelika ignored him.

"I didn't say that!" said Noah.

"But you're acting like it!" said Angelika.

Uh-oh. This was out of control. He had to do something.

"Hey, uh—broccoli!" he hissed.

Noah and Angelika stopped squabbling and stared at Finch.

"Somebody needs help," he said, "and it doesn't matter which one of us figures it out. It's not a contest!"

That's what his mom and dad said when he and Sam were fighting. And he hated when they said that—because it basically *was* a contest with him and Sam. But this shouldn't be a contest between Noah and Angelika.

"It doesn't matter which one of us figures it out, 'cause we're on the same team," he said. "Right, guys?"

Noah and Angelika were quiet for a little bit. Deciding.

Finally, Angelika asked, "Like Green Team?"

"Like Green Team," agreed Finch. "Except we're not about recycling. We're about finding out who buried the note."

Angelika agreed. "Okay," she said.

"Okay," echoed Noah. "Except we need another name— not Green Team."

Angelika's hand shot up. "I'll think of something," she said. "I'll come up with a name."

"Awesome!" said Finch.

"Whatever," said Noah.

"But I still don't get why anybody would bury a note,"

said Angelika. "Because how would that get you any help?"

Finch had thought about this a lot. Maybe the kid who needed help didn't want anybody to know. Maybe whoever it was needed it to stay secret.

"Burying the note was like making a wish," he said. "Whoever did it didn't want anybody to know. But they still need help. Which means we've gotta find out who it was, and what kind of help they need, and then give it to them, in secret!"

His mom's voice carried through the library. "I need all of Mrs. Adler's students to be lining up and checking out their books!"

Finch scrambled up and headed for the end of the line. Now that he had started looking, he saw problems everywhere, multiplying, like . . . lice! It made his head itch, just thinking about it.

But inside his itchy head, Finch was making a list:

- Figure out how to help the kids whose problems they already knew about.
- Then investigate all the other kids, and try to help them, if they needed it.
- And the whole time, keep the peace between the two kids who were supposed to be helping him.

Busted

Finch called a meeting. Friday. Recess. Playground. They sat on the green grass freckled with yellow dandelions.

"Can we decide on our team name first?" asked Angelika. "Remember, you said I could come up with a name? So, I have three ideas. And we can vote on them, okay?"

"Umm, sure," said Finch. "Let's hear them."

Angelika sat with her knees hugged to her chest, her green Crocs bobbing up and down as she rocked back and forth. "First, Candy Stripers. That's what they call people who volunteer in hospitals. My mom did it when she was young, and now she's a nurse."

"Hate it," said Noah. "No offense."

"You didn't tell your mom about the note, did you?" asked Finch.

"Of course not!" said Angelika. "I can keep a secret!"

"Okay, sorry," said Finch. "So, go: next idea?"

"Shleep Team!" said Angelika.

Noah burst out laughing. "What?" he cried. "*Sheep*?"

"No," she said. "*Shleep*. It's the letters of 'helpers,' rearranged. And it rhymes, like Green Team. And it's cool because nobody will know what it means. Like if we say, 'See you later for Shleep Team,' they won't know what we're talking about!"

Noah was still laughing, and Finch was trying not to.

"What happened to the R?" he asked. "There's an R in the word 'helpers.' "

"I had to leave it out," said Angelika. "It's not perfect," she admitted. "And my last idea is Cake Club. It stands for Caring Kids, because there's a C for caring and a K for kids in the word cake. If we want to have a meeting we can say, 'Are you going to have cake later?' Get it?"

"I get it," said Finch. "I like it. Cake Club!"

"Shleep Team!" said Noah. "That's my vote. Shleep!" He said the word like a sheep baaing. "*Shle-ee-ep! Shle-ee-ep! Shle-ee-ep!*"

"I vote for Cake Club," said Finch.

"Well, I like Candy Stripers," said Angelika.

"*Shle-ee-ep!*" baaed Noah. "*Shle-ee-ep!*"

Finch was beginning to understand why his dad got mad when nobody would "stay on track" during a conversation at supper. "How about we decide our name later?"

"*Shleep!*" spluttered Noah, cracking himself up.

"Stop saying that!" ordered Angelika. "Finch, make him stop!"

"Come on, Noah," said Finch. "Cool it."

But Noah had got the giggles. He kept saying *shleep* until finally Finch dug the tin box from his pocket and held it out in the palm of his hand. "Earth to Noah," he said. "Remember what's in here?"

Noah stopped joking around. "The note."

"The note," said Finch, nodding. "So, what did you guys find out?"

Noah made his report. He had found out that Oscar and Oliver would stop shaking down David for milk money, if somebody else paid them off.

Angelika had learned that now Graciela had head lice, too.

Finch hadn't made any progress figuring out Atticus. But he had found out a bunch of other stuff. Yesterday he'd been having another friendly chat with the social worker (more questions and more one-word answers and more "Awesomes!"), and he had been looking at all the drawings on the wall. And there was a drawing of a really cool dog with three heads, like they'd read about in Greek mythology, and it was signed in the corner: *Kael*.

Also, Millie was on the same list he was on—kids who hadn't finished their times tables—and she needed to finish, to keep Mrs. Adler from having a serious talk with her parents about her math placement for sixth grade.

And Mohamed was obsessed with reading every single *Captain Underpants* book.

"So now what?" asked Angelika.

"Now we try to help them," said Finch, "in case any of them was the notewriter."

"That's kinda lame," said Noah. "No offense."

"I know," admitted Finch. "But we need to do *something*."

"Or we need more clues," said Angelika.

"Like what?" asked Noah.

"Like *that*," she said, pointing to the Band-Aid tin that held the note.

The three of them stared at the box and then, as if they'd all had the same idea at the same time, they all began talking at once.

"Maybe there's another one—"

"Where the first one came from—"

"In the garden—"

They scrambled up and set off running across the dandelion-speckled grass. They sped past kids roaming the playground, kids climbing on the spiderweb, kids playing foursquare on the blacktop, over to where the garden plots were laid out. And where, right in the middle of the plot for Mrs. Adler's class, stood a skinny kid with sandy, shaggy hair.

The Atticus who went by Atticus.

"Hey!" said Finch.

Atticus turned around with a startled look on his face. "Uh . . . hey."

Uh-oh—now what? Finch couldn't imagine coming

right out and asking *Did you bury a note here? Do you need help?*

"What's up?" he asked instead.

"Nothing," said Atticus. He popped something green in his mouth and munched it.

"Whatcha eating?" asked Noah.

Atticus held out a handful of snow peas. "Want one?"

Noah took one but Angelika hesitated.

"Did you get permission?" she asked.

"Of course," said Atticus, sounding a little mad. "Grammy Mary said I could. Go ask her!"

"Sorry," she said, taking a peapod. "Thanks."

"Thanks," echoed Finch. He took a peapod from Atticus, checking out the palm of his hand and making a note in his mind: *clean*. Not the hand of a kid who had been digging in the dirt. He ought to know.

"Later," said Atticus, and ambled off.

They waited until he was out of earshot.

"That was weird," said Angelika.

"Definitely," agreed Noah.

"He wasn't burying anything," said Finch. "His hands were totally clean. I checked."

"But there was something funny," said Angelika. "Like he didn't want us to know what he was doing."

"We need more clues," said Noah. "Maybe we should look in his locker."

"No way," said Finch. "Too dangerous. Last time I tried that I got sent to Mr. White's office."

"Busted!" said Noah, grinning.

"Which kind of served you right," said Angelika.

"Yeah, but now he thinks there's something wrong with me," complained Finch. "He tried to get me to tell him what was going on, and he was asking all these questions. But I didn't tell him anything."

"Hey," said Noah. "Hey, *Finch*."

Finch ignored Noah. He wasn't done complaining. "He was all, like, I am *Awesomeraptor*. But I'm, like, *more* awesome."

"Finch, hang on," said Noah.

Finch didn't hang on, because he was on a roll. "I am the fierce and mighty *Finchosaurus!*" he shouted as he leapt, landing in a fierce and mighty dinosaur pose.

"Busted," said Noah again. Not grinning.

Angelika lifted her hand in a wave. "Hey, Mr. White," she said.

Finch froze. He froze in his fearsome dinosaur pose. The pose where he was a fierce dinosaur, more awesome than *Awesomeraptor*.

"Hello, Angelika!" said Mr. White. "Hello, Noah. Hello, Finch. What's that you're doing—karate?"

"Umm . . . no," said Finch. Unfreezing, he let his arms fall to his sides. "I was . . ." He trailed off, trying to think of a good answer. Then he decided he might as well tell the truth. "I was making believe I was a dinosaur."

"He's nuts for dinosaurs," added Noah.

Angelika chimed in, "He wants to be a paleontologist."

"I never told you that!" said Finch.

"Everybody knows that," she said with a shrug.

"So that's all we're doing," said Noah. "Talking about dinosaurs, and paleontology."

"Paleontology," said Mr. White, tapping his finger to his white beard in a thinking-about-it pose. "Interesting. Is that why you like to dig so much, Finch?"

Uh-oh. *Awesomeraptor* was on the prowl. But Mr. White wasn't going to trick him into saying too much. Finch gave a one-word answer.

"Yep," he said.

That didn't stop *Awesomeraptor*.

"Did you know that all you need to start a club here at Acorn is one adult adviser and three kids? So, if you three wanted to start a club for kids interested in paleontology, I'd be more than happy to help. What do you say?"

Unfortunately, Noah and Angelika didn't seem to see that *Awesomeraptor* was stalking them.

"I know!" cried Angelika, as she waved her hand in the air. "I know, I know! Let's call it Paleo Pals!"

Noah looked as if he thought this was the funniest thing ever. "Paleo Pals," he said, grinning. "Love it!"

With a big smile on his face, Mr. White pounced. "Finch? What do you think?"

Finch thought fast. First thought: No way!

Second thought: Paleo Pals could be a good cover. He and Noah and Angelika could *pretend* it was a club for kids interested in paleontology, but they would know the truth—that they were actually, secretly, still looking for the kid who needed help.

"Let's do it," he said.

Welcome to Maine

"Why can't we bring Whoopie Pie?" asked Finch. "Gammy loves Whoopie Pie."

"What about allowance?" asked Sam. "We still get our allowance tomorrow, right?"

"Buckle up, boys," said their mom to Finch and Sam in the backseat. And to their dad she asked, "Ready for five hours of this?"

Finch buckled up, then touched the tin box in his pocket. Safe. His investigation would have to wait, though. It was Friday afternoon and they were headed to Maine for the long weekend.

Finch's dad backed down the driveway. "Yes, Sam, you will get your allowance tomorrow. And Mrs. Duncan will check in on the cat. She'll be fine, Finch."

Which didn't answer Finch's question. "Why can't we bring her?"

Sam elbowed Finch in the side. "You," he whispered. "Me. Tomorrow. Don't forget." Then he stuck in his earbuds and closed his eyes. Checking out.

Finch hadn't forgotten the deal he'd made with Sam. He just hadn't figured out how to get out of it. Which he needed to do, because he needed that money for Oscar and Oliver, so they would stop taking David's milk money.

The car rolled slowly down the leafy street. Turned a corner to a bigger street. Fewer trees. More cars. Going faster.

"Gammy loves Whoopie Pie," said Finch again.

Gammy was the one who had named the cat, because he was black with a little bit of white on his throat, the same color as a whoopie pie.

"Finch," said his dad, catching his eye in the rearview mirror. "Settle down."

Finch's mom twisted around in the front seat, so she was facing Finch. "Gammy loves the cat, but she's not at the house, remember? She's at Pine Grove."

Finch nodded. He remembered. Gammy was in the nursing home.

"And we're going to be busy visiting her," said his mom, "and helping Guppy."

"Helping how?"

"Helping him get organized."

"Is that why Dad's coming?"

Finch's dad came along to Maine sometimes, but not always. But getting people organized was his specialty. His whole job was helping people declutter and downsize and move. Most of his clients were old people, leaving the house they'd lived in for a long time.

"Yes, Guppy will be moving to an apartment in Pine Grove, so he can be closer to Gammy. And Dad can start helping figure out what goes where."

"Is he moving *now*? This weekend?"

"No," said his mom. "The apartment needs a fresh coat of paint. But we can look at it now to help us decide which furniture will go to the new place, and which furniture needs to go . . ." she trailed off. "Somewhere else," she finished.

"What about this summer?" pressed Finch. "Will he move before our summer vacation?"

"Finch," said his dad. "This is not about you."

"It's okay, Les," said his mom. "Finch, no matter when Guppy moves, we'll still go up this summer. He won't sell the house right away."

"Sell the *house*?" cried Finch.

His mom took a big breath. "I don't have all the answers to all your questions, Finch. But, yes. Someday they will sell the house. Any more questions?"

Finch shook his head, no, and his mom turned around. Soon his dad zoomed up the ramp onto the highway. Finch watched the big green highway signs sweep past, naming the towns, and then the states. Connecticut, Massachusetts, New Hampshire, Maine. Somewhere after the *Welcome to Maine* sign they ate the supper his dad had packed—tuna-fish roll-ups—and somewhere after that, Finch fell asleep.

When he woke up, it took him a second to figure out where he was. Then he smelled his favorite smell in the world: low tide. Salt and mud.

He was in Maine. He had fallen asleep in the car and now it was Saturday and he was here. He scrambled out of bed and hurried downstairs—"Why does he always *galumph* down the stairs?" he heard his father say—and ran over to his grandfather for a hug.

Guppy squeezed Finch tight, then stepped back, still holding him by the shoulders. "Let me look at you."

"I'm as tall as you," said Finch.

"You grew," agreed Guppy, nodding. "And I shrunk."

Finch looked around to see if anything else was different. Luckily, nothing. Finch liked this house just the way it was. Six chairs, painted green, circling the dining table. A pantry with jars of jam on one shelf, cans of soup and tuna on another, and the bottom shelf full of games. And the door frame where Gammy had marked his and Sam's height every summer.

It was weird how kids got taller and taller, and old people got shorter and shorter. He never heard of anybody keeping track of your height going down, though. Nobody wanted to make a big deal about *that*.

Finch was as tall as Guppy now, but still not taller than his dad. Yet. At school, Finch knew which guys were about the same height as him: Kael and Khalid and Mohamed. He knew Noah and Oscar and Oliver were taller. And David and the Atticus who went by Atticus were shorter.

He was pretty sure Gammy was shorter than him now, too, but it was hard to tell because she was sitting in a wheelchair when they saw her. He had to hunch over for a hug.

"Whoopie Pie says hi," he said.

Gammy smiled. "You tell Whoopie Pie I said hello, too."

The place where she lived smelled like Brussels sprouts. Which was not a smell Finch liked. He was glad when they took her outside. He and Sam took turns pushing the wheelchair along the path that wound through the tall pine trees. Then they all went to see the apartment Guppy was moving into, next door to the nursing home. Finch's dad measured everything and took pictures on his phone. Finch's mom walked around saying things like, *Your big comfy chair could go here. The table would fit there if we take out the extra leaves. Not room for six dining chairs, though.* Finch was glad when they left there, too.

Next stop was the grocery store. They filled up a carriage with food, and went through the checkout line.

"Dad," said Sam. "Dad, it's allowance day, remember?"

"Yes, Sam," said their dad. "I remember." He got cash back from the lady at the register, gave five dollars to Sam and five dollars to Finch and made the same joke he always did.

"Don't spend it all in one place," he said.

Sam didn't shake down Finch right away. He waited as they drove out of town. Crossed the big bridge. Zoomed down the long stretch of road through the marsh, with water on either side. Their mom and dad were in the front seats, talking about furniture. Finch was in the worst seat—the middle of the back—with Sam on one side and Guppy on the other, dozing off.

He felt Sam's elbow dig into his ribs, and then Sam was holding out his hand, palm flat. The silent signal for *Give me my money. Now.*

From his pocket, Finch scrounged out his brand-new five-dollar bill and forked it over. He didn't exactly blame Sam. Sure, it was blackmail, but Finch had made a deal. Still—making a deal didn't mean he wanted to see his brother's triumphant grin. He turned his head the other way, toward Guppy. Who wasn't dozing anymore. He was wide awake, staring at Finch with a puzzled look on his face.

Digging Clams

"Mom," said Finch, balancing on one foot. "Mom," he echoed, standing on the other foot. "Mom," he said, hopping from foot to foot—one word per hop—"Mom, Mom, Mom, Mom, Mom!"

"Finch, stop!" said his mother. "What part of 'Wait a minute' don't you understand?"

Finch stopped saying *Mom*, but he kept hopping. "I *am* waiting," he said. "That's what I'm doing."

"Finch," said his dad. "Less hopping, okay?"

"But it's low tide," said Finch.

"I know that," said his mom, "and so does your grandfather. Just—*wait*."

Finch *was* waiting. Except he didn't get why people said, *Let's go,* and then they said, *Wait a minute.* It was like saying *go—no, stop.* When Finch wanted to go-*go*. He wanted to get out on the mudflats and start digging. This was his first chance, because yesterday, when they'd gotten back from Pine Grove, the tide was high.

Finch had done a report on the tides in fourth grade—written *and* oral. In front of the whole class, he had explained how it was all about the moon. As the earth rotated, all the places in line with the moon felt the tug of its gravity. The moon's gravitational force field actually *pulled* all the water on earth *toward* the moon. That was high tide—when the place you were in was in line with the moon.

But the earth was always turning, so pretty soon that same place wasn't lined up with the moon's force field. Soon that same place was where all the water was being pulled *from*. That was low tide.

Then he had described the tidal bay where his grandparents lived—how at low tide you could go out onto the bay's muddy bottom. You could walk around in a place that was deep underwater when the tide was high.

At the end he had asked, "Does anyone have a question or a comment?"

Noah had raised his hand. "How fast does the water come in? Is it like a tidal wave?"

No, explained Finch. The tide came in slowly, more like a bathtub being filled. It took about six hours for the tide to go out, and six to come back in.

Waiting for his grandfather now, Finch kept hopping. Because even if the tide wasn't going to pour in like a giant wave, it wasn't going to stay out forever. It was low tide *now*, and he wanted to get going. He was still hopping when

Guppy appeared.

"Who's ready to dig some clams?"

"Me!" said Finch.

"It's just you and Finch, Dad," said Finch's mom. "Les and I are going to stay here, and Sam's still sleeping, if you can believe it."

They found the clam-digging rake and a bucket from the shed, and walked the short distance from the house to the shore. They picked their way over prickly crabgrass. Climbed over slippery, seaweedy rocks. Crossed the shallow channel of water at the edge of the bay. Then, finally, Finch was out in the middle of the mudflats. He wasn't sure if the flats were more like sandy mud, or muddy sand. Either way, it was mud you didn't sink into. Mud you could dig. It was excellent mud.

Finch plunked himself down. He didn't mind getting dirty. He would use his hands and Guppy could use the rake.

"Wait!" said Guppy.

"*What*?" groaned Finch. *More waiting?* What now?

"Hold on," said Guppy. "Before you get your hands dirty, I've got something for you." He reached into his back pocket, pulled out a five-dollar bill, and handed it to Finch. "Looked to me like you're going to be a little short this week."

"Wow," said Finch. "*Thanks*." He shoved the money in his pocket.

"You're welcome."

They began working. Wherever a clam's airhole dotted the mud, Guppy stuck in the rake and flipped it out, scooping up piles of mud. Searching through the piles, Finch picked out any clams and put them in the bucket.

"Aren't you going to ask why I gave Sam my allowance?"

"Nope."

"You don't want to know?"

"I do," said Guppy. "But only if you want to tell me."

Overhead, a seagull flapped across a bright blue sky. It dropped a shell onto the rocks, trying to crack it open to get at what was inside.

When he first found the note, Finch had pictured himself figuring it out all by himself. Then he got a couple of helpers, Noah and Angelika. And that was cool. Even Sue Hendrickson didn't try to dig up *Tyrannosaurus Sue* all by herself, right?

But now, Guppy?

Guppy had given him five dollars, no questions asked. And Guppy lived here, in Maine. He wasn't going to butt into stuff at Acorn. Except, what if Guppy told his mom and dad? Finch still didn't want them to know. If they knew, they'd probably tell Mrs. Adler. She'd probably make all the kids go talk to Mr. White, or something. The whole thing would get taken away from him, before he'd had a chance to figure it out.

"If I tell you, will you promise not to tell Mom and Dad?" asked Finch.

Guppy was quiet for a second. Thinking.

"Tell you what," he finally said. "I can't agree to keep a secret from your mom and dad. But I can agree to a . . . surprise-in-progress. If you plan on telling them yourself, someday."

Finch picked another clam from the mud. It was funny: Finding something in the ground was the beginning of the story. Except clams just lived in the mud. They weren't buried there by somebody else. But maybe after Finch had figured out whoever that somebody else was, he could tell his mom and dad. That was a fair deal.

"I found something," he said.

"You found a big one," agreed Guppy.

Finch dropped the clam into the bucket. "No," he said. "Something else."

He started with yesterday—giving Sam his allowance so Sam wouldn't sit with him at lunch, like their parents wanted him to. When he got back to the day he was just trying to put a worm in the school garden, he ran over to the channel of water to wash the mud off his hands. He pulled the tin box from his pocket and took out what was inside.

Peering at the scrap of paper, Guppy read aloud. "*Help.*"

"I'm going to find out who wrote it."

A giant grin lit up Guppy's face. "Sounds like one of Gammy's mysteries she likes so much. And you're going to get to the bottom of it!"

"Me and my friends," agreed Finch.

"Outstanding," said Guppy. "And I wouldn't mind a report now and then. You could give me a call once in a while, right? Tell me how it's going?"

"Absolutely," said Finch. "I'll call you as soon as I know something."

Bonus Points

"*Good morning,*" said Finch, "*and welcome back to Acorn Comprehensive. We hope everyone had a great holiday. Today is Tuesday, May 29. Hot lunch will be mashed potato bowls.*"

Ten minutes ago, Mr. White had nabbed Finch in the school lobby with "awesome news!" He had gotten the paleontology club fast-tracked and he wanted Finch to make the announcement. In the office, Mrs. Stuckey had asked if he would like to read all the morning announcements? Definitely! said Finch. And she'd handed him the piece of paper he was reading from.

"*Acorn Comprehensive is starting a new club: Paleo Pals. It's for any students interested in paleontology. First meeting is today, after school, in the library.*"

The library! *Awesomeraptor* and *Momosaurus*, teaming up! Not great news, but Finch didn't have time to think about that now. He had to keep reading aloud.

"*Also, because of the Monday holiday, Green Team members will be checking recycling bins today.*"

Finch thought fast. Later today he'd be roaming around. And anybody on Green Team could roam around with him. And while they were checking out recycling boxes, he could be checking *them* out. He kept talking, but he wasn't reading aloud anymore. He was making it up.

"*Green Team is always looking for new members. So, if you're interested, see Miss Kirby or any of the kids on Green Team.*"

He got back on script.

The last words on the paper were just: "*Birthday wishes: Phoebe Collins.*" Finch had no idea who Phoebe was, but he wanted to make this good. The way he wanted it to sound when it was his turn.

"*Finally,*" he said, "*on behalf of the whole Acorn Comprehensive community, we want to wish a very. Happy. Birthday. To . . . PHOEBE COLLINS!*"

Mrs. Stuckey took the microphone and switched it off. "Thank you, Finch," she said. "That's plenty of announcements for today."

"Is that true, Finch?" asked Mr. White. He was standing with the arms of his blue-and-white-checked shirt crisscrossed over his chest, as if what he'd just heard was making him cross, for real. "Green Team is looking for new members, *now*?"

Finch thought fast again. He didn't actually know if that was true, but why couldn't it be?

"Probably," he said. "You're starting a new club with only three weeks to go. So why can't kids join Green Team now, too?"

Just then somebody dashed across the lobby, past the yellow construction-paper Sunshine Awards taped to the wall around the giant construction-paper oak tree, and into the office. Miss Kirby!

Miss Kirby was one of those not-a-teacher helpers, like Grammy Mary. Except she wasn't old. She had just graduated from college. Her job at Acorn was anything and everything to do with nature and the environment, like Green Team, and the class gardens.

"I heard the announcements," she said. "Great job taking the initiative, Finch!"

Finch wanted to give Miss Kirby a Sunshine Award!

"No problem," he said, with a little good-bye wave.

In a hurry—he wanted to ask Atticus to join Green Team—he sped down the hall as fast as he could without getting called out for running, and bounded into Mrs. Adler's room.

"Good morning, Finch," said Grammy Mary, with her big smile.

"Hey, Grammy Mary," said Finch. "Sorry I'm late, Mrs. Adler, I—"

"We know," said Mrs. Adler, holding up a stop-talking hand. "We heard the announcements. And you already have two volunteers for Green Team." She turned her stop-talking hand into a look-over-there hand, pointing to two kids with their hands in the air: Mohamed and Fatouma.

Okay, thought Finch. Plan A was Atticus. Plan B, Mohamed and Fatouma.

After lunch, he took them to Miss Kirby's office. A bunch of fourth graders and some kids from the other fifth-grade class were there, waiting for their assignments.

"Hey, Miss Kirby, this is Mohamed and Fatouma. They're joining Green Team."

"Welcome!" said Miss Kirby. "No Noah today?"

"No Noah today," said Finch. "He's busy."

He didn't say exactly what Noah was busy doing: He was on the playground, getting Finch's allowance to Oscar and Oliver.

Miss Kirby began explaining how they always went out in pairs, or a group of three if there were an odd number of kids. "So, it looks like we have eleven kids today."

Fatouma's hand shot in the air. "Five teams," she announced. "Four teams of two kids, and one team with three."

"Thank you, Fatouma!" said Miss Kirby. "And with five teams inspecting eighteen classrooms, how many rooms will each team inspect?"

Fatouma thought for a second. "Three teams will do four rooms—that's twelve. And two teams will do three rooms—that's six. That's eighteen."

"Nicely done," said Miss Kirby, handing out their badges and clipboards. "Finch, why don't you and Mohamed and Fatouma be our three-person team?"

The three of them headed out. Their first classroom was empty. No kids and no teacher, either.

"Can I hold the clipboard and write stuff down?" asked Fatouma.

"Sure," said Finch.

He handed her the clipboard and began digging through the bin. He picked up a piece of paper with somebody's multiplication table for the number 7, and suddenly remembered: Millie. And just as suddenly, saw the answer: Fatouma.

"Hey, Fatouma, want to do me a favor?"

"I guess," she said.

"You know Millie?" he asked.

Fatouma nodded.

"She needs help with her times tables. You wanna be, like, her study buddy?"

"Does she want me to?"

"Well," said Finch, "she doesn't exactly know I'm asking you. But I heard she needed help, and you're so good at math. Maybe you could help her."

Waiting for her answer, Finch looked at Fatouma. He realized he didn't know much about her. He thought she hung out with a few girls on the playground, but he didn't know who her best friend was, or if she even had one.

"Okay," said Fatouma. Inside her blue hijab, a smile lit up her face. "Sure!"

"Awesome," said Finch. "Let's give this room ten points."

In the next room, he and Mohamed got to work, digging through the bin. Mohamed started looking harder at each piece of paper, too.

"Hey," he said, holding up a drawing of a horse with wings. Inside a speech bubble were the words *Nothing escapes my eye!* "Can I keep this?"

Finch shrugged. "Sure," he said. "How come?"

"I'm going to take it to comics club and show Mrs. Haywood."

"There's a club for comics?"

"Kind of," said Mohamed. "Mrs. Haywood is here early every day, and she lets anyone who wants come to her room and draw. Most kids draw comics."

Finch felt like his brain was working way faster than it ever did in Mrs. Adler's class. Because he had just thought of something else. The drawing of the three-headed dog he had seen in Mr. White's office, with the name in the corner: *Kael.* He wondered why Kael had to go see Mr. White. Maybe it was like Finch going just because he had looked in Angelika's locker and dug a bunch of holes in their class garden. They thought something was wrong with him, even though there wasn't. Or maybe Kael did have a problem.

Either way, he was an excellent artist.

"Hey," he said. "Does Kael ever go?"

Mohamed shook his head.

"Can you ask him if he wants to? He's really good at drawing."

"What's up?" asked Fatouma. "You trying to get a Sunshine Award?"

"No," said Finch.

Mohamed asked, "Then what are you doing?"

Finch didn't want to lie; he just didn't want to tell the whole truth. Even though he had put Noah and Angelika on his crew, and let Guppy in on the secret, he still didn't want everyone to know.

"Maybe it's a little like a Sunshine," admitted Finch. "But it's not official. I'm just trying to . . . do some favors. So, can you ask Kael if he wants to go to comics club sometime, and I'll do a favor for you, okay? I'll ask my mom to order all the *Captain Underpants* books the library doesn't have."

"Really?" asked Mohamed. "You can do that?"

"Yeah, I can," said Finch, leaving out the fact that he didn't get any special treatment just because the librarian was his mom. Any kid could ask her to get more books. "Definitely," he added.

"*Yes!*" said Mohamed. "Okay, I'm in."

Next room, next bin, overflowing with cardboard milk cartons and pieces of paper written on both sides.

"Let's give them ten points plus a couple bonus points," said Finch.

Fatouma wrote 10 + 2 on the clipboard. "You should ask Khalid, too," she said. "He's really good at drawing *Star Wars* characters."

"Kael and Khalid," said Mohamed. "Got it."

Bonus points, thought Finch, as they headed back to turn in their clipboard. In one Green Team outing he had signed up Fatouma to help Millie, Mohamed to help Kael and Khalid, and himself to help Mohamed.

Next stop, Paleo Pals.

Paleo Pals

They streamed in—a bunch of kids who were in aftercare, looking for something new to do, and a bunch of kids who could have gone home, but who thought Paleo Pals sounded fun. Besides Noah and Angelika from his class, there were Oscar and Oliver, some fifth graders from Mrs. Tomlinson's class, and a bunch of kids in third and fourth. No older kids. And not Atticus, unfortunately.

"Hello, everyone," said Finch's mom. "And welcome to your library. Mr. White asked if Paleo Pals could meet in here and I said I'd be delighted. We've got a big assortment of books on paleontology over here on these tables. At the end of your meeting, you can either come to the desk and check them out, or leave the books right where you found them, okay? Enjoy!"

Mr. White gave a little wave of his hand to Finch's mom. "Thank you, Mrs. Martin, for welcoming us to your space. I'm sure we'll do our best to leave the library as nice as we found it."

If there was one thing Finch hated, it was grown-ups telling you what to do by having a pretend conversation with another grown-up.

"Now," said Mr. White, "I've been working on finding some activities so we can really *dig into* paleontology." He paused to give kids time to laugh at his joke, then added, "But in the meantime, here are some mazes and word searches." He began passing out a stack of papers and a box of pencils.

"Mr. White, Mr. White!" said Angelika, waving her hand. "Can we vote on who's going to be president?"

"President?" asked Mr. White. "Umm . . . yes, great idea, Angelika. Let's do that right now."

Noah waved his hand in the air. "I nominate Finch!"

"I nominate Oscar!" shouted Oliver.

"I nominate Oliver!" shouted Oscar.

"Any other nominations?" asked Mr. White. "Good."

He passed out more paper for ballots, and when the votes were counted, he said, "I am pleased to announce that your Paleo Pals president is . . . Finch Martin!"

Everybody clapped and hollered—because clapping for somebody was an okay way to make a lot of noise—and Finch jumped up and took a bow, imagining this moment in a book. *Finch Martin—discoverer of* Finchosaurus, *the largest dinosaur ever to roam the earth—was elected president of his local paleontology club at the age of ten.*

After the clapping died down, Finch grabbed a *Do Not Disturb: Student Reading* sign and signaled to Noah and Angelika to meet him at one of the smaller tables. Paleo Pals wasn't turning out too bad. But he had more important things to do than mazes and word searches.

"Let's talk about *cake*," he said.

"Cake?" asked Noah. "Tell me your first cool president thing is getting us cake for snack."

"Not 'cake,' " whispered Angelika. "*Cake.* Remember? Caring kids?"

"I *know*," said Noah. "I'm just kidding. But seriously, President Finch, are we getting snacks here?"

"Seriously," said Finch. "I have no idea. But did you deliver the money?"

"What money?" asked Angelika.

"My allowance," said Finch. "I gave it to Noah to give to Oscar and Oliver, at recess."

"Mission accomplished," said Noah.

"No way!" said Angelika.

"Yes, way," said Noah. "Because I am a caring kid. Who deserves some cake."

"No, I mean, no way—because *I* gave them money, *too*. I didn't know you were going to!"

Finch, Noah, and Angelika all swiveled around in their seats to look at Oscar and Oliver, who were both giving them the two-thumbs-up sign, big grins on their faces.

"Oops," said Noah.

"That's not fair," said Angelika. "They are such bullies. We should tell."

"No, we shouldn't," said Finch. "You know if we tell on them they will take it out on David, for*ever*. Let's just do better telling each other stuff. Like, here's what I did today."

As he told them what happened during Green Team—who was doing what, to help who—Angelika was busy circling things on a "Dinosaur Discovery" word search. When he was done talking, she held up the paper. Instead of circling whole words, like *fossil* and *carnivore*, she had circled single letters. D. M. K. K.

"I get it," said Noah. "David. Millie. Kael. Khalid. What about A for Atticus?"

"No," said Finch, shaking his head. "We've investigated him, but we don't have a plan to help him. We don't even know if he needs any help."

"Alert," whispered Angelika. "*Alert.*"

The grown-ups were wandering the room, going from table to table.

"Hello, Noah," said Finch's mom. "Hello, Angelika. Hello, Finch. Or should I say, President Finch?"

"You can call me Finch," said Finch.

"All right," she said. "How's it going? Anything I can help you with?"

"Yes," piped up Angelika. "I was wondering, do you

have any books about lice? Like, how to get rid of them?"

Finch's mom had a funny look on her face. An I'm-not-freaking-out look. An I'm-a-librarian-helping-a-student-use-our-resources look.

"We have a wonderful book called *The Giant Book of Parasites*, which I believe has a chapter on head lice," said Finch's mom. She pointed to the Dewey Decimal poster. "So, where do you think you would find that book?"

Angelika studied the poster. "On the shelf with the five hundreds?"

"You got it," said Finch's mom.

"And Mom?" said Finch. "I mean, Mrs. Martin? You know the *Captain Underpants* books? Does the library have all of them?"

"Probably not every single one," she said.

"But could you get them? I mean, would you—please?"

"I can do that," said Finch's mom, nodding. "I can add some to my next book order, and I can borrow some from other schools."

"Thanks," said Finch.

"How about you, Noah? Anything I can help you with?"

"I was wondering if there was going to be snacks?" asked Noah.

"I will talk to Mr. White," she said. "I'm sure we can get some snacks in for the next meeting. In fact, I'm going to ask him right now."

She headed off, and Angelika circled four more letters. M for Mohamed. C for Charlotte, H for Haley, and G for Graciela.

"Your mom is awesome," said Noah. "Look how many kids we just got help for. I'm gonna go find a book so I can do a *Who Loves This Book? Noah Does!* recommendation for her."

Angelika said, "I'll go find that book on parasites."

Alone, Finch checked the letters Angelika had circled on the "Dinosaur Discovery" word search. It was almost half the class. He had no way of knowing if any of them was the notewriter. Or if any of the things he and Angelika and Noah were doing was going to actually help anybody, notewriter or not. But it was better than nothing. Way better.

He still wanted to be known someday as *Finch Martin, discoverer of* Finchosaurus, *the largest dinosaur ever to roam the earth*. But that was going to take a while. For now, this was good. For now, he was Finch Martin, president of Paleo Pals. Finch Martin, president of "Cake Club."

And Finch Martin—*not* the kid getting all the extra help anymore. The one giving it.

The Fruits of Our Labor

The next day was as hot and muggy as dog breath.

Grammy Mary sat on one of the big boulders alongside the garden. She wore a straw hat with a giant plastic purple flower on the brim. "Good morning, Finch," she said with a smile.

"Hey, Grammy Mary," said Finch. "Cool hat."

"It's keeping me cool," she said, taking it off and fanning herself.

"Fifth graders!" called Mrs. Adler, raising her hand in the air for silence. "Let's give our full attention to Miss Kirby."

"Good morning, everyone," said Miss Kirby. She was wearing short overalls, like a cross between a farmer and a little kid. "Because of this heat, we're only going to work outside for about thirty minutes. Then we'll go in and make a salad from the greens we're going to harvest. Who here wants to eat some kale?"

That wasn't a real question, because the whole class garden thing was being willing to at least *try* eating the food they grew. So everybody raised their hands to show they would eat kale.

"Then let's get gardening!" said Miss Kirby, and began assigning different kids to different jobs.

Finch sidled up to Noah. "Let's split up," he whispered. "I'm gonna talk to Atticus."

"Check," said Noah. "I'll hang with David."

Finch grabbed a trowel and went over to where Atticus was cutting leaves and putting them into a bowl. "Miss Kirby said I could weed," he said. "What's a weed, again?"

"What's a weed?" echoed Atticus. His face scrunched into a worried frown. "Weeds are the plants we don't want."

"I get that," said Finch. "I mean, *where* are the weeds?"

"*Oh*," said Atticus, his frown switching to a grin. "This is kale," he said, pointing to a row of plants with dark green curlicue leaves. "And all this other stuff is weeds." He pointed to clumps of green here and there. "Weed. Weed. Weed."

"Got it," said Finch. He stuck his trowel into the ground, yanked up a weed, and tossed it aside.

"You're supposed to make a pile," said Atticus. "Remember? For the kids collecting stuff for the compost? Miss Kirby says a weed isn't edible but it can still help us make edible things."

"Who says it's not edible?" asked Finch.

"Umm . . . Miss Kirby?"

"But is that true?" asked Finch. He dug up another

clump of weeds, bit off a mouthful, and chewed.

"How is it?" asked Atticus, staring at Finch as if he was doing a magic trick.

Finch swallowed. "I'm gonna go with not edible," he said.

Atticus cracked up, laughing. "Too bad you're not a cow. Then you could eat it."

"Too bad I'm not an herbivorous dinosaur," said Finch.

"*Diplodocus*," suggested Atticus.

"Or *Iguanodon*," said Finch.

"Totally," agreed Atticus.

Finch kept digging and tossing the weeds into a pile. Dig, yank, toss. Dig, yank, toss. He should have talked to Atticus a long time ago. Not because of his investigation; just because the kid was pretty fun. Why hadn't they ever hung out before?

Maybe because he was already hanging out with Noah, pretty much 24/7. They hung out during school. And they hung out after school.

Simple—except it got Finch thinking. If a kid did something different than you after school, you *might* be a during-school friend. But maybe not. Best friends were usually the kids you saw after school, too. Over the years, Finch had done different things, but whatever he had done, it was almost always with Noah.

"All right, Mrs. Adler's fifth graders," called Miss Kirby. "Time to get out of this heat."

Finch and Atticus lined up to rinse their hands with the hose, then trooped inside to the Activity Room—out of the dog-breath air and into the air-conditioning—where everybody had to wash their hands again using soap. Miss Kirby asked for a few helpers to wash and cut up kale. Everyone else could have free time at one of the quiet tables.

Finch saw Angelika volunteer to make salad, along with Charlotte, Haley, and Graciela. He followed Atticus, who beelined it for one of the smaller tables. There was a stack of books and the usual assortment of mazes, puzzles, and word searches.

"Hey," said Noah, as he plopped down in a chair beside Finch. "We've got a problem."

"Hey," said David, as he took another seat.

David was one of the shorter-than-Finch kids. He was so short that when he sat down his head was barely above the table. He had super-curly hair that he let grow long, kind of like camouflage: *I'm bigger than I look!*

"Hey," echoed Finch. "What problem?"

"They want more money," said Noah.

"Money?" asked Finch, trying to play dumb. And trying to signal Noah: *Why are you talking about this in front of everyone? Remember how this was kind of a secret?*

"Oscar and Oliver took your money," explained David, giving Finch a funny look, as if he really *was* dumb. "And now they say they want more!"

"Sorry," said Noah, with a shrug. "But he basically guessed."

"Guessed what?" asked Atticus.

Finch didn't answer right away. For a second, he held on to the used-to-be-all-his secret. But what was the point? Noah and Angelika and Guppy knew everything. Fatouma and Mohamed knew he was trying to do favors for kids, even if they didn't know why. And now David knew they were trying to help him. So why not tell Atticus?

Besides, he was mad. Too mad to worry about keeping secrets. In a low voice, he explained: How he'd found a note that said *Help*. How they thought David might need help because Oscar and Oliver were taking his milk money. How Noah had given money to Oscar and Oliver. How they'd taken money from Angelika, too. And how now, apparently, they wanted *more* money.

"That stinks," said Atticus. He sounded mad, too.

"Totally," agreed David. "And I didn't even write the note! And now you guys are out all that money, and it's my fault."

"No," said Finch firmly. "It is not your fault."

"I know!" said Noah. "I know how to get more money. I'll charge kids to see my bare feet."

"I always wanted to see your toes," said Atticus.

"Me, too," said David. "Are they really stuck together?"

"I've seen them," said Finch. "You don't want to pay

money for that. Seriously."

Everybody laughed, and Finch joined in. "But seriously," he said again. "We're not gonna let them shake you down. I get allowance again on Saturday."

"I have a better idea," said Atticus. "When do they get you?"

"Recess," said David.

Atticus leaned forward. "So, we make sure you're never alone at recess. One of us is always with you."

"Really?" asked David, sitting up a little straighter.

"I'm in," said Noah.

"We're all in," said Finch.

He held out his fist, and Noah, David, and Atticus all bumped their fists against his.

Miss Kirby began tapping a spoon against a big bowl. "Grammy Mary, can you tell us what time it is?"

Grammy Mary looked in the bowl. "I think it's time to eat the fruits of our labor," she said.

"Yes," agreed Miss Kirby. "Everybody please line up and get ready to try a delicious vegetable."

Finch got up and stood in line.

"I hope you love it, Finch," said Miss Kirby as she handed him a bowl of kale salad.

Finch took the bowl, seriously doubting he was going to like it. Maybe if he was an herbivorous dinosaur he might. But he wasn't. He took a nibble. Disgusting! It was worse than the weeds he had eaten, trying to make Atticus laugh.

That got him thinking about Atticus again. Atticus had turned out to be funny. Atticus had turned out to have a good idea for how to help David. Most important, nothing Atticus had said seemed like he might have a reason to bury a note that said *Help*. But when David said he hadn't written the note, Atticus didn't say, "Me neither."

"This is poison," said Noah. "I'm dying."

"Me, too," said Finch, hoping that Miss Kirby's definition of "trying" really did mean one bite, and not "cleaning your plate." Glancing around, wondering where to dump out the rest of his salad, he saw Atticus. He was shoveling kale into his mouth with a strange look on his face.

The look didn't say *Disgusting*. But it didn't say *Yum*, either. It just said *Hungry*. Like he was going to eat that bowl of kale, no matter how it tasted.

Martin Martin

Finch woke up Saturday to the smell of pancakes and the sound of a baby crying. Pancakes meant that his parents were starting the day with a big breakfast because it was going to be a clean-the-house Saturday. Everybody would have to do their fair share. A baby crying meant . . . he had no idea.

He ran downstairs to see what was going on.

"Mom, how do I make it stop?" asked Sam, holding the crying baby. It wasn't a real baby. It was one of the make-believe ones the health teacher gave to eighth graders. "I already fed it and burped it and changed its diaper. That's everything on the checklist."

"Change its *diaper*?" asked Finch. "Does it—you know—go poop?"

"No," said Sam, wearily. "You just change the diaper and somehow the software knows. It keeps track of everything you did or didn't do."

"Does this baby have a name?" asked Finch's dad from

where he stood at the stove, cooking pancakes.

"Martin," said Sam. "His name is Martin."

"Martin?" cried Finch. "So, it's *Martin Martin*? That's funny!"

Their mom reached out for the baby. "I'll hold him for a little bit. Hello, you sweet thing," she cooed.

The baby stopped crying. In the silence of no-crying, the warm air coming through the open window was suddenly filled with bird chirps.

Sam plunked himself down in a chair and rested his head on the table, using his arm for a pillow. "I'm so tired," he groaned. "He kept crying in the night."

Finch's dad added another pancake to the platter on the table. "You cried when you were a baby, too."

Finch put a pancake on his plate. "Did *I* cry?"

"Of course," said their mom. "That's one of the ways babies communicate. Our job as parents is figuring out what you're trying to say. Sometimes babies are hungry. Sometimes they just want to be held."

Finch smeared butter and poured maple syrup on his pancake. "What did I want?" he asked, before he took a big bite.

Finch's mom and dad laughed.

"What's so funny?" he cried, his mouth full of warm, sweet pancake.

"You wanted to *move*," said his mom. "You liked being jiggled."

"And you liked being outside," recalled his dad. "I took you outside. And then jiggled."

Finch jiggled a little in his chair, because jiggling still felt good.

"What did I like?" asked Sam in a muffled voice, face-down in the crook of his elbow.

"Eating," said their mom. "And sleeping. You were the most marvelous sleeper."

"Sleeping now," he said.

The baby began crying again and Finch jumped up from his chair. "Can I try? Maybe he likes being jiggled."

Finch's mom held out the baby and Finch took him in his arms. His body was all bundled up so the only thing that showed was his little face, the golden-brown color of maple syrup. He tried jiggling, and Martin Martin stopped crying.

"You're a natural," said his dad as he flipped a pancake.

"I'm *Maiasaura*," said Finch. "The good mother dinosaur."

"I'm going back to bed," said Sam.

"Hold your horses," said their dad. "It's Saturday. We're doing chores."

"What about the baby?" asked Finch.

"Maybe the baby will sleep," said their mom. "Or maybe Sam can find a babysitter."

"I'll do it!" said Finch. "Sam, want to hire me?"

"How much?"

Bird chirps flew in on the warm air, while Finch thought.

Then he grinned at his brother. "I'm thinking, five dollars?"

Sam stared at Finch with a look Finch didn't see too often. *Outsmarted.* Finch wasn't going to be blackmailed out of his allowance this week!

"For the whole day," countered Sam.

"Deal," agreed Finch.

"Whoa," said their dad. "Isn't Sam supposed to be responsible?"

"Finding child care *is* being responsible," pointed out their mom.

"I don't know," said their dad, shaking his head. "Isn't the point of bringing home these babies to learn that you're the one on duty, twenty-four/seven?"

"No," said Sam. "The point is, I needed extra credit in health class."

"How can you need extra credit in *health*?"

"I'm going to be honest with you, Dad," said Sam. "I did *less* work than I should have."

"Very funny," said their dad. "But all right, fine. Finch is babysitting. You think five dollars is fair?"

"Too late!" crowed Sam. "He made a deal."

"It's okay," said Finch. "I'm cool with five dollars." Still holding the baby, he slid back onto his chair. Martin Martin stayed quiet, and Finch gobbled the rest of his pancake to the sounds of birds chirping and cheeping.

"It's something to think about, boys," said their mom.

"You care for a child yourself, or you pay somebody. Or, if you're lucky, you find somebody like Noah's mom."

"What about Noah's mom?" asked Finch.

"We traded child care," she said. "You knew that."

Finch was so surprised he stopped eating. "No, I didn't."

"Of course you did," said his mom, wrapping her hands around her mug of coffee, a puzzled look on her face. "You know how, if you weren't in aftercare, you either went to Noah's, or he came here, right?"

"Yeah," he said. "Because he's my friend."

"You were already friends in kindergarten," agreed his mom. "And it was lucky you kept on being such good friends, because we both needed child care after school."

She went on, talking about how back when Noah's mother was a stay-at-home mom, they almost always went there. Then Noah's parents divorced and his mom went back to work, so they had gone to school aftercare, remember, in third grade? In fourth grade the grown-ups decided that they could go to one of their houses, if they stuck together. Finally, this year the grown-ups agreed that fifth graders were old enough to go home alone, if they wanted.

"So, you've graduated, I guess," finished his mom. "No more child care for you. Now you're the one doing the child care!"

"Way to go," added his dad.

"Way to go," echoed Finch. "Yay, me."

But Finch wasn't feeling all *Way to go—yay, me.* The way his mom had described the last few years was true, he guessed. He'd just never thought about the reason why. Or, the fact that his *why*—he and Noah were friends—was totally different from his mom's *why.* Glorified babysitting. It was like looking at a picture book you thought you knew by heart, and finding that the caption said something totally different.

He felt like a lot of things were starting to look different, ever since he had found the note. Things looked the same on the outside. But underneath, it was a different story. How far beneath the surface did you have to go, to get to the bottom? Which reminded Finch—Guppy was waiting for a report.

"How goes it?" asked Guppy. "Any luck getting to the bottom of your mystery note?"

"Not really," said Finch, sitting cross-legged on the grass with Martin Martin, Sam's health class make-believe baby, in his lap. He had taken the phone outside so he could talk without other people hearing. "It's like, the more I dig, the farther away the bottom gets." He told his grandfather about the kids he'd talked to that week. "But I don't know if any of them wrote the note."

"I suppose everyone needs help with something or other," said Guppy. "Except me! You can tell your mother not to worry about me. Tell her I'm fine, will you?"

"Okay," said Finch. "How's Gammy?"

"Well, it's a funny thing, now that I think of it. She was the one who helped others all her life, and now she's the one being helped. Sometimes it makes her grumpy."

Finch got that. He had felt grumpy back when everybody was trying to help him all the time.

"Finch, I have to tell you something. Gammy was having a bad day and I was trying to take her mind off things, and I told her about your mystery note. She was so excited! I hope you're not mad?"

"That's okay," said Finch, looking down at the make-believe baby in his lap. Little Martin was quiet now. But if he was crying, Finch would want him to stop. Just like Guppy would want to stop Gammy from feeling grumpy. "It's cool."

Guppy said he was sure Finch would figure it out soon, and Finch hoped that was true, because there wasn't much time left. It was June—only two and a half weeks of school to go.

In a Blur

The next week went by in a blur.

On Sunday, Finch offered to babysit again—*if* his brother gave him more money. Ten dollars.

"Ten dollars?" cried Sam, just as Martin Martin began crying. "All right, whatever," he said, handing over the baby. "I heard you need it for a good cause, anyway."

"What did you hear?" asked Finch.

"That you're stopping two kids from messing with another kid." Sam made a fist and thumped Finch on the shoulder. "So that's cool."

On Monday, he had Green Team with Noah. They looked at all the papers in all the recycling bins. Nothing.

On Tuesday at Paleo Pals, he and Noah and Angelika sat together at one of the small tables with a *Do Not Disturb: Student Reading* sign and went over the class list again.

For starters, they crossed off themselves. *Angelika, Finch,*

Noah. Because it wasn't them. Obviously. Then they crossed off the kids they had at least tried to help. *Charlotte, David, Graciela, Haley, Kael, Khalid, Millie, Mohamed.* That left *Atticus*, still a mystery. *Fatouma*, who was helping Millie but not getting any help herself. *Oscar* and *Oliver*, who Angelika said shouldn't count. And *Quinn* and *Samantha*, who they still needed to check out.

On Wednesday, Finch challenged Atticus to a game of rock, paper, scissors. For a second, Atticus looked surprised. Then he made a fist and in unison they chanted, "Rock, paper, scissors, shoot!"

Finch was paper. Atticus was scissors. Scissors cut paper.

"I win," said Atticus.

"Two out of three?" asked Finch. "And if I win, you answer a question, okay?"

In answer, Atticus held out his fist.

Finch tried paper again, and Atticus picked rock. Paper covers rock. They were tied.

Third round. Finch was rock. Atticus was scissors.

"Rock smashes scissors," admitted Atticus. "You win. So, the answer is No."

"I didn't even ask the question!"

"It's about the note, right? The one you found? The reason we're guarding David at recess?"

"Yeah," said Finch.

"It wasn't me. I mean, I guess I could have written it . . ." Atticus trailed off, then finished with, "But I didn't."

On Thursday, Mr. White invited Finch for a little chat in his office.

"How's everything going?" he asked. "How is *Finch*?"

"Good," answered Finch, swaying from side to side. Because if he had to sit still—on a regular chair, inside— he at least had to *move*.

"I should get one of those bouncy-ball chairs in here," said Mr. White. He stood and offered Finch his seat. "Want to switch?"

Finch hopped onto Mr. White's chair. *Nice*. You could scoot around on the wheels. You could swivel back and forth, or even spin in a whole circle. How come grown-ups got such nice chairs, and kids didn't? That was another not-fair thing about being a kid.

"That's a cool drawing," he said, pointing to the picture of the three-headed dog, with Kael's name in the corner.

"It is," agreed Mr. White. "Do you like to draw? Mrs. Haywood is here early most mornings for kids who want to use the art room. I hear there's a few boys your age going now."

Uh-oh. *Awesomeraptor* on the hunt.

"That's okay," Finch said, swiveling back and forth. "I don't really like drawing."

Mr. White nodded. "And you're already pretty busy,

111

aren't you? Green Team. Paleo Pals. How do you think Paleo Pals is going?"

Finch couldn't resist. "Awesome!" he said, spinning in a complete circle.

"Good," said Mr. White, giving him a funny look, as if he knew Finch was making fun of him. "Any ideas for how it could be better? Activities you'd like to do? Maybe a field trip?"

Finch stopped spinning and swiveling, and worrying about *Awesomeraptor* on the prowl, and blurted out exactly what he thought. "Dinosaur State Park!"

"Dinosaur State Park," echoed Mr. White. "Sounds like an awesome idea. I'll pencil it in for next fall, see if I can make that happen."

On Friday, he got a chance to hang out with Noah, just the two of them. *If* Noah wanted. Finch wasn't sure what to think, ever since his mom had explained about the grown-ups swapping child care. He knew what *he* thought: Noah was his best friend. But what did Noah think? Finch couldn't imagine actually asking him. That'd be weird. But maybe he could find out.

"Hang out?" he asked Noah after school. Their usual shorthand. No need to bother with full sentences.

"Duh," said Noah.

Finch grinned. Question answered. That's what he liked

about being friends with Noah. You got to the bottom of things in about one second.

"My house?"

"Can't," said Noah, shaking his head. "Dog patrol."

Noah spent half the week with his mom and Penny the poodle, and half the week with his dad and Rozzy the chocolate doodle. But no matter which house Noah was going to, he might be on dog patrol, because both dogs were old. The kind of old where they would have an accident if they were left in the house too long.

"Okay, yours," agreed Finch.

He walked alongside Noah under a hot blue sky. Other kids were walking, too. Little kids with grown-ups, and older kids by themselves. Block by block, kids peeled off, down side streets. Finally, they got to Noah's house.

Finch dropped his backpack and got ready for a big chocolate doodle slobber. But nobody jumped up to slobber him. Rozzy lay on her bed in the corner of the kitchen, thumping her tail on the floor.

Finch knelt down and scratched Rozzy in her favorite scratching spot, behind her ears. "What's the matter with her?"

Noah's face was scrunched up, like he was trying not to cry.

"The usual," he said. "She's old. It's just gotten worse in the last few days." He got up and held open the door. "Come on, Rozzy."

Rozzy turned her big brown eyes to Noah with a look that said *I can't*.

Noah came back over to the dog's bed and grabbed two corners. "Come on, help me."

Finch got the other two corners. Together, they managed to tug the cushion—with Rozzy atop—outside. They set it down on the grass. Rozzy rose and walked shakily a few feet away to pee, then wobbled a few more feet and lay down.

Finch and Noah lay on the lawn, too. Not going anywhere. Overhead, the blue sky was broiling hot. Underneath, the green grass was cool. Finch felt like the filling in a sky–grass sandwich.

He didn't know why he said what he said next. It just popped out.

"My grandmother's old. She had to go live somewhere else."

"They should have, like, doggy nursing homes," said Noah.

"They should," agreed Finch, knowing that they didn't. When dogs got this old and this sick, they didn't go to a nursing home. They went to the vet. And they didn't come back.

His grandmother wasn't coming home, either. And someday Guppy might leave, too. And then their house would be sold. He couldn't imagine it. Some other family living there. During Green Team he went around visiting his old classrooms, but who cared that new kids were there now? He had moved on.

He had never imagined moving on from the house in

Maine, though. He'd thought that was forever.

Just as Finch was thinking that he didn't want to think about *forever* anymore, or dogs—or people—getting old, Noah asked, "Want to see my toes?"

Which was a perfect Noah thing to say.

"Definitely," said Finch.

Noah kicked off his shoes and lifted a foot up in the blue sky. The fourth toe and the pinky toe were stuck together.

"What did one toe say to the other toe?" asked Finch, like he always did, and together they delivered the punch line: "Stick with me!"

Trick Question

One week of June melted into another. Inside Acorn Comprehensive, teachers were teaching as fast as they could, trying to wrap things up before the end of the year. Outside, the grass was growing like crazy. Grown-ups kept cutting it, filling the air with the roar of mowers mowing and the smell of grass, and lopping off the dandelions' yellow heads. But the dandelions kept growing right back, popping open in the sun.

Finch was outside, running in circles around his mom, who was mowing the lawn. His bare feet were turning green from the grass. It was the Sunday before the second-to-last week of school. And the very last one wasn't even a full week; this was the home stretch!

"Finch!" called his dad from the back porch.

Finch didn't feel like stopping. He waved and kept circling the yard, his feet turning greener and greener.

People used to think dinosaurs were green, like alligators. Or maybe brown. But nobody really knew. They might have had feathers. They might have been red, or blue, or yellow. Or maybe they *were* green. That was one of the things he wanted to find out, when he was a real paleontologist.

"Finch!" called his dad again.

The sound of the mower stopped.

"Finch," said his mom. "Your dad's calling you!"

"I can't stop!" shouted Finch, still running, "I have green feet! I'm out of control!"

"Less running, Finch," said his dad. "More stopping. Now."

There was something in his dad's voice that Finch didn't like. Finch's mom must not have liked it either. She left the mower in the middle of the yard and followed Finch over to the back porch.

Finch's dad was holding his phone. "I got an email from Mrs. Adler," he said.

"Unfair!" groaned Finch.

His parents had told him what it was like when they were kids. First of all, they weren't the kind of kids teachers sent notes home about. But if they *had* been, the notes would have gone home in the kid's lunchbox. Or, if they were extra important, they would have been delivered by the mailman. Either way, a message from the teacher wouldn't pop up on a Sunday afternoon, when you were trying to turn your feet green.

"She says you haven't handed in a lot of work."

"*What?*" asked Finch's mom.

Peering at his phone, Finch's dad read aloud, "Finch is missing a number of assignments, including his twelve-times test, his *You Were There in Colonial Connecticut* essay, and his acrostic poem. He should know that if he fails to complete all his work there will be consequences."

"What kind of consequences?" asked Finch's mom.

"Well, a bad grade, obviously," said Finch's dad, still staring at the message on the phone. "Also, not being allowed to go on the class trip."

"*What?*" cried Finch. "She can't do that!"

Finch's brother pushed open the back door and came outside. "Can't do what?"

"Stop me from going on the fifth-grade trip!"

"She stopped Aidan Doyle from going when I was in her class," said Sam. "He had to spend the day with Mrs. Stuckey in the office."

"But what's going on?" asked his dad. "Why haven't you handed in these assignments?"

"Dad, I've been really busy!" said Finch.

"Busy?" asked his mom. "Doing what?"

Uh-oh. Trick question. Finch *had* been busy. Just not busy doing homework. He felt frozen, which hardly ever happened, because he wasn't a guy who froze. He was the guy who couldn't stop bouncing off the walls.

Still frozen, Finch hadn't answered his mom's question, which was usually a big no-no. But now his parents began talking to each other as if he wasn't even there.

"I thought this year was going okay, wasn't it?" asked his dad.

"I thought so, too," agreed his mom. "Ever since Mrs. Davison got him his special seat."

"And Mrs. Adler said his work met the standard, at our last conference, remember?"

"He *was* meeting the standard."

There were three grades you could get. Exceeds the standard. Meets the standard. Needs improvement.

In kindergarten, Finch hadn't needed any improving. Kindergarten was just Mrs. Murphy, letting kids "dance their wiggly-jigglies out." If another grown-up came around it was for something fun, like art.

It wasn't until first grade that the teacher decided he wasn't meeting the standard. That's when he learned about special services. And it wasn't that he didn't like Mrs. Hunter, the speech therapist, or Mrs. Davison, the occupational therapist. He just didn't like leaving the classroom, where his friends were. Which was why he liked the bouncy seat Mrs. Davison got him at the beginning of the year. Bouncing was as good as digging. Bouncing helped him "settle down." By the time parent–teacher conferences came around in November, he had gone from *needs improvement* to *meets the standard*. And then all the extra help had stopped. Which was fine by Finch.

"And now he clearly isn't doing well," said his dad. "Which makes me wonder. Maybe they shouldn't have stopped all the services he was getting."

"We've talked about this," said his mom. "Teachers don't usually recommend services for kids who are doing okay. They need to be struggling, which Finch isn't anymore. Or *wasn't*. Until now."

"I'm not struggling!" blurted Finch. "I don't need extra help!"

His parents stared at Finch like they'd forgotten him. In the silence, they could hear the jingle-jangle sound of the ice-cream truck cruising the neighborhood.

"Can we get ice cream?" asked Sam. "Mom, can we? Last time you said no, but you said that next time we could. This is next time, right? So, can we?"

As usual, Sam was trying to get the attention away from Finch and onto him. Which for once, Finch didn't mind. He flashed his brother a grateful smile. Distraction! Changing the subject! Nice.

Sam being nice gave Finch a good feeling. A warm, dandelion-springing-back-in-the-sun feeling.

Turning to his parents, he said, "Hey, less frowny faces! More smiley faces!"

A funny noise started coming out of Sam. He was hooting with laughter.

Finch's parents were not laughing.

"I am not amused," said his mom.

"Neither am I," said his dad. "And neither is Mrs. Adler. She says you have until the end of the week to hand in the missing assignments, or no trip."

"It's not that big a deal," said Sam, coming back to his defense. "All we did was go to the water park, and all the picnic tables had bees. And Asa Steinberg got stung and he was allergic and had to go to the hospital."

Grateful, Finch chimed in. "It's no big deal," he said. "I don't care if I miss the trip."

"Does it say where they're going this year?" asked Finch's mom.

"Let's see," said Finch's dad, scrolling through the note from Mrs. Adler. "Oh, no!"

He stopped talking and made a face. Definitely not a smiley face. More of a frowny face. But not a mad frowny; more like a shocked-and-scared frowny.

"What?" asked Finch.

"I think you'll want to go on this trip," said his dad.

"Go where?" demanded Finch. "Dad, where are we going?"

F for Fidgeter

"Dinosaur State Park," said Finch's dad.

"Dinosaur State Park!" shouted Finch.

He took a giant leap off the back porch and ran around the yard once. Then he ran all the way around again. And again. Finch hadn't been there for a year, ever since they closed for renovations. They'd had the fossil tracks of a dinosaur, and who knew what else they might have by now?

"Finch!" called his mom, waving him in.

Finch circled back to the porch.

"Dinosaur," he said, panting. "State. Park."

"Yes," said his dad. "Like Mrs. Adler said—if you finish all your work."

Iffosaurus. If you had been listening. If you had thought of that. If you finish all your work.

"That's not fair," said Sam. "Finch would want to go there more than anyone. He's the president of Paleo Pals!"

"Life isn't always fair," said his dad, and began to launch into his lecture on fairness.

Life wasn't fair, if by "fair" you meant that everybody got treated the same way. Some people had it harder than others. Some people had it easier. That was life.

But it was fair, if by "fair" you meant that there were consequences for not following the rules. That was the essence of fairness.

"Dad, stop!" said Finch. "I know all that already."

"Well, I hope you know we're on your side," said his mom. "We really hope you can go. But it's up to you."

"Mom, I know!" said Finch.

"And do you know what you have to do?" asked his dad.

"Dad, I know!"

"Well, do you think you can do it?"

Another trick question: Could he do all his homework? He couldn't tell his parents *No*, because then he'd be in trouble for not even trying. But he couldn't tell them *Yes*, because the truth was, he didn't know. It was a lot of work. Plus, he had a lot of other stuff to get done. He tried slipping in between *Yes* and *No*.

"I'll do my best," he said.

That's what grown-ups always said they wanted you to do: your best.

Apparently, they didn't always mean it.

"Your *best*?" roared his dad. "I don't want to hear any nonsense about you doing your *best*! Just get it done!"

"Okay, okay!" said Finch.

"Okay, *what*?"

"Okay, I'll do it!"

"Good," said his dad, pointing to the back door. "You can start by getting cracking on that poem. Kitchen table. Now."

Whoa—Finch's dad hardly ever went all *T. rex*. Finch figured he better do what his dad said. He headed inside, got a pencil and a piece of paper, and sat down at the kitchen table.

The screen door opened and closed as his dad came into the house.

"Don't mind me," he said. "I'm just cooking supper."

Finch gave a *whatever* shrug. Because his dad couldn't go all *T. rex* on him and then expect him to be friendly.

"We're having roast chicken and mashed potatoes," said his dad. "You like that, right?"

Staring down at the piece of paper, Finch gave another shrug and the tiniest answer possible. "I guess," he said.

"Hey," said Finch's dad. "Listen, I'm sorry I snapped at you. I knew how much going to Dinosaur State Park would mean to you, and I guess I was scared you might miss out."

Hearing his dad say *Sorry* made Finch feel funny. It made him feel the opposite of frozen, like he was melting. It almost made him want to say . . . everything. Say, *I don't need extra help, but somebody else does.* But he couldn't. He wasn't going to give up now, just so he could go on the field trip.

"Bottom line," said his dad, "I shouldn't have raised my voice. That's not going to help you write a poem, is it?"

Finch shook his head. No.

"All right," said his dad. "Supper's in about half an hour. Let's see if you can make some progress by then, okay?"

Finch picked up his pencil, and his dad began peeling potatoes. Outside, the roar of the mower started up again. It wasn't fair. His dad *liked* cooking. His mom *liked* working in the yard. Grown-ups got to do whatever they wanted. Finch did *not* like writing poetry. Especially poetry about himself. He got up to sharpen his pencil. Then he sat down. Then he got up to put some cat food in Whoopie Pie's bowl.

"Finch," said his dad, with a potato in one hand and a peeler in the other. "Can you settle down and get to work?"

Finch sat down. He took a banana from the fruit bowl.

"Finch," said his dad. "It's almost supper."

"Mom said fresh fruit was okay, no matter what. That's the *rule*."

Finch's dad took a deep breath, like maybe he was trying not to turn into *T. rex* again.

"Mom did say that," he admitted. "Okay."

Victory! Finch ate the banana as slowly as he could. Then he got up to put the peel in the compost bucket.

Finch's dad drew another big breath. "Here's another rule," he said. "Sit down. And sit still. For *five. Whole. Minutes.*"

"That's not a rule," argued Finch. "A rule is, like, for all the time."

"True," said Finch's dad. "This is more like an *order*. Sit. Down. Now."

Finch sat back down, picked up his pencil, and wrote the letter F. He tapped his pencil on the paper. F, F, F, F, F.

"Less fidgeting, Finch. More thinking," said his dad.

That gave Finch an idea.

F was for *Fidgeter*, as in, Stop fidgeting!

Yes! One letter down, four to go. Except Finch didn't think he could really use *Fidgeter* for his first word. Not in a real poem. But it was more fun to write a funny poem. A poem that didn't count. Nobody ever had to see it, right?

Next letter: I. I was for . . . *Impish!* Finch remembered that word from a book his mom used to read to him. To be *impish* was to be like an *imp*—a little mischief maker.

Finch laughed out loud when he thought of the word for the letter N.

N was for *Nincompoop*. It had the word *poop* in it! Nincompoop, nincompoop, nincompoop!

"How's it going, buddy?" asked his dad.

"Good," answered Finch.

C was for . . . he didn't know. He tapped his pencil, trying to think. He couldn't think of anything. All he could do was smell the scent of roasting chicken floating through the kitchen. *Chicken* started with a C. Maybe he should write that down.

C was for *Chicken*.

It was funny. How come the word for a bird you ate was the same as the word for being afraid? Were chickens really afraid?

Tapping his pencil on the paper, Finch thought *chicken* might be a good word for him. Not the bird part; the afraid part. Because he didn't want to do this poem for real. He didn't want to *dig deep*. Because what if he dug deep inside himself and found some words, and nobody liked the poem? What was there special about him, anyway? He was just a fidgeting, impish, nincompoopy chicken.

The screen door opened and slapped shut, and his mom came into the kitchen. The smell of cut grass came with her.

"Well, this is a nice picture," she said. "Dad cooking supper and Finch writing a poem!"

Finch didn't tell his mom she had the picture all wrong. The caption wouldn't be *Finch writing his acrostic poem*. The caption would be *This is Finch, who failed to do his homework and did not get to go on the trip to Dinosaur State Park, even though he probably wanted to go more than anybody in the whole entire fifth grade.*

His mom took a seat and leaned toward Finch. "Let's see what you've got."

"Mom, no!" he shouted, spreading his hands over the paper. "You can't look. It's—confidential!"

Finch held still, breathing in the smell of freshly cut

grass and roasting chicken, while his mom studied him with a making-up-her-mind look on her face. Grown-ups talked about things being confidential all the time. But would his mom buy the idea that he didn't have to show her his poem because it was *confidential*?

"Okay," she finally said, with a smile. "I hope you'll show me when you're finished. But I'll give you some space for now."

And then she backed off. She and his dad bustled around, setting the table, talking and laughing. And giving him space. All because they thought he was doing his homework.

Which gave Finch an I for Idea.

Olden Days

The next day was the first day of the second-to-last week of school, and Finch had a plan. Tell everybody he was going to do his best, and then pretend he was doing his best. And then everybody would leave him alone, and he could keep doing what he wanted—trying to discover who wrote the note.

He had to find out before fifth grade was over, and everybody scattered for the summer. For one thing, he didn't want the year to end with a big note on his report card: Needs improvement. Recommend services in sixth grade. He wanted it to end with him being Finch Martin, the kid who helped somebody. Finch Martin, who did something important.

And for another thing, Guppy and Gammy were waiting for him to get to the bottom of the mystery.

First thing Monday morning, Finch put his plan into action. He told Mrs. Adler he was going to do his best to finish all his work.

"I'm very glad to hear it," said Mrs. Adler. "I'll expect to see you in this room, in your seat, every day at recess and after school. Are we clear?"

Uh-oh—no recess was going to cut into his investigation time. Finch did his best to act like he didn't mind.

"Totally clear," said Finch, nodding. "Recess and after school. I'll be here."

He told Miss Kirby and Mr. White, too. Because "doing his best" for Mrs. Adler meant that he couldn't show up for the last Green Team or Paleo Pals—the club Mr. White had basically started just for him. But Miss Kirby said it was fine, and Mr. White said it was awesome, pumping his fist in the air. "Dinosaur State Park, here you come!"

Whoa—Mr. White actually seemed to care.

"Dinosaur State Park, here I come!" echoed Finch.

Mrs. Adler, off his back: check. Miss Kirby: check. Mr. White: check. Finch didn't feel too bad about pretending to them. The only grown-up he felt bad about was Grammy Mary.

"Good morning, Finch!" she said on Monday morning.

"Hey, Grammy Mary."

"Welcome back, Finch!" she said, when he came back from the cafetorium after lunch, to spend recess in the classroom.

"Hey, Grammy Mary."

"Hi, Finch!" she said at the end of the day.

"Hey, Grammy Mary," he said.

All the kids had gone, and Mrs. Adler had left for a meeting. It was just him and Grammy Mary.

"I know you have some catching up to do," she said, giving him her big Grammy Mary smile. "What are you going to work on this afternoon?"

"I don't know," he said, rolling back and forth on his bouncy-ball chair.

He rummaged through the cubby that hung beneath his desk, searching for the *If you finish all your work* list Mrs. Adler had given him. Other papers, a pencil, another pencil, an eraser shaped like a *Stegosaurus*—ooh, cookie—and there! The list. He handed it to Grammy Mary.

"Let's see," she said, smoothing out the sheet and reading aloud. "Pass your twelve-times test, finish the *You Were There* essay, and write the acrostic poem. And let's see, since every piece of paper has two sides . . ." Trailing off, she turned the paper over. "Good news, Finch. Nothing on this side."

Finch laughed. He'd always known Grammy Mary was nice, but he hadn't realized she was funny, too. Even though he saw her every day, the only thing he knew about her was her favorite color: purple. She almost always wore something purple. Today she was wearing a lavender shirt with a picture of a horse galloping off into the sunset.

"You really like purple, don't you?"

"It's my go-to color," she said, nodding. "But let's not get sidetracked! What are you going to work on now?"

Finch switched from rolling back and forth to bobbing up and down. He felt bad because Grammy Mary was so nice. And he wanted to go to Dinosaur State Park—of course he did! But there was no way he could finish all of his missing assignments, so why even bother?

Besides, he had more important things to do. He put his hand in his pocket to touch the tin box where he kept the folded-up note. Who had written it?

Finch bobbed up and down: Was it one of the kids they had already tried to help?

And up and down: Or was it one of the kids they hadn't gotten around to helping yet?

And up and down and up and down, and suddenly, he stopped bobbing up and down. Because suddenly, he knew who might know.

"Hey, Grammy Mary—you know all the kids in our class, right?"

Grammy Mary nodded. "Of course," she said.

Maybe it was silly to ask about Atticus. He'd already said he hadn't written the note. But it seemed like maybe he needed help anyway. It seemed like he was hungry—not just the way Finch felt starving sometimes, before he ate. Hungry, for real. Some kids got free lunch, and Finch hoped Atticus was one of them. But what about before and after school?

"What about Atticus? Do you know, like, anything about him?"

"I know that Atticus is a delightful boy," said Grammy Mary.

Finch pressed. "Do you think he's, like, okay?"

Grammy Mary took a deep breath, as if she was trying to decide what to say. Or not say. Finally, she said, "I think Atticus is going to be just fine."

Going to be just fine wasn't the same thing as *Fine now*, but Finch got the message. He knew she was thinking about Atticus, and probably so were other grown-ups. And that's all he was going to get out of Grammy Mary.

"Now," she said, in a moving-right-along tone. "Let's talk about your essay on colonial Connecticut. How is that coming?"

"It's partway done," said Finch.

Partway done meant he had the first sentence. "I am ten years old and I live in Connecticut in 1786."

"Do you and your friends ever play 'Olden Days'?" asked Grammy Mary.

"Sometimes I pretend I'm a dinosaur," admitted Finch.

"That's really olden days!" she said, laughing. "Well, when I was a little girl I had a friend, and her grandmother lived on a farm. My friend would visit in the summer, and take me along. And we used to *love* making believe we were little girls living a long time ago, maybe in the colonial era—we didn't really know. But when there were no cars or telephones."

Bobbing lightly on his bouncy chair, Finch listened as Grammy Mary told him all about the farm. Pouring a little bit of water into an old hand-pump well to get it going. That was called "priming the pump." Collecting horse chestnuts from a tree that was more than a hundred years old. And cooking pancakes in a cast-iron frying pan that had belonged to the grandmother of the friend's grandmother.

"Just think," said Grammy Mary, holding out her hand. "This hand touched a skillet that had been touched by the hand of somebody who had *really lived in olden days*."

She looked at her hand as if it was something magical, and then she laughed a little tinkling laugh, like the song from the ice-cream truck.

"And those pancakes were *so good*," she went on. "Do you like pancakes?"

"I totally like pancakes," said Finch.

They talked about different toppings for pancakes, and whether the people in colonial Connecticut might have had them. Maple syrup—yes. Raspberry jam—probably. Chocolate chips—no!

The door opened. Mrs. Adler was back. Grammy Mary smiled and waved good-bye. Finch waved back and picked up his pencil. He might as well have fun with this, too, like the poem.

I was born in Connecticut on June 19—that part was actually true—*in 1776. On my next birthday I will be eleven. For my birthday, my mother will cook my favorite food, griddle cakes. I like them with butter and maple syrup. My mother makes the butter with milk from our cows. My father makes the maple syrup with sap from our maple trees . . .*

Mrs. Adler began wiping the whiteboard clean. "I'm glad to see you on task, Finch," she said. "Keep up the good work!"

Mrs. Adler looked so happy—which was not how she usually looked when she looked at Finch—that he got a funny feeling in his stomach. She thought he was trying his best, not goofing around, writing about pancakes. What was she going to say when she found out that his "best" was just a big act? *If I had known you were only pretending to do your best, I would have . . .* what?

The way he saw it, he had a good reason. But he doubted *Iffosaurus* was going to see things his way.

Thump

The cafetorium smelled like fish sticks. Finch pushed his tray down the lunch line. He got fish sticks and carrot sticks and a carton of milk. Noah, right behind him, got fish sticks and carrot sticks and a carton of milk. At the end of the line, Finch stood, scanning the cafetorium, wondering where he should sit.

"Come on," said Noah. "What are you waiting for?"

"We should split up," said Finch. "We should sit with kids we haven't helped yet."

"No," said Noah. "We should sit together and I should quiz you on your twelves. Because don't you want to go to Dinosaur State Park?"

"Of course!" said Finch. "But we're running out of time!"

It was Tuesday, the second day of the second-to-last week of school. Finch only had until this Friday to hand in all of his missing assignments. But, more important, he only had one more week until the last day of school.

One more week to find the writer of the note.

"Never mind that," said Noah. "Seriously. You gotta help yourself! Who am I gonna sit with on the bus if you're stuck in the office with Mrs. Stuckey?"

Across the cafetorium, the teacher's aide on lunch duty pointed at them, in the school signal: Do what you're supposed to do or I'm coming over there. In other words: *Sit down.*

"Look," said Finch. "I'm stuck in Mrs. Adler's room every single day for recess and after school. This is the only time I have for investigating. And this is important. Shleep Team, right?" He made a noise like a sheep baa-ing. "*Ple-ee-ase.*"

"Okay, okay!" said Noah, laughing. "Who's left?"

"Oscar and Oliver."

"*No way!* Why would we try and help them? They were shaking down David for milk money *all year*, until we stopped them."

"I know that," said Finch. "They're bullies. But it still could have been one of them, couldn't it? Being a jerk doesn't mean you don't need help with anything."

"Okay, okay, here I go," said Noah, and made his baa-ing noise. "*Baa-baa.* Get it? Bye-bye? *Baa-baa?*"

"Bye-bye," baa-ed Finch, looking around for who else was left on the list.

Bingo! Quinn and Samantha were sitting together. He went over to their table and set down his tray.

"Hey," he said. "Can I sit here?"

Quinn nodded and Samantha scooted over on the bench seat to make room for him.

They usually spent recess French-braiding each other's hair, so they kind of looked alike, with long blonde braids crisscrossing their skulls and running down their backs, like a spiny-ridged dinosaur.

"What's up?" asked Samantha. "You fighting with Noah?"

"No!" he said.

"Then how come he's sitting with Oscar and Oliver?" asked Quinn.

Finch thought fast. "Uh . . . Green Team!" he said. "We're trying to sign kids up for next year."

"You should join," said Samantha, pointing a finger at Quinn.

"I don't know," said Quinn. "Maybe."

"Talk her into it," said Samantha to Finch. "Next year. Okay?"

"Sure," agreed Finch.

"Promise?" asked Samantha.

"He doesn't have to promise," said Quinn. "I'll do it if I feel like it!" She picked up her tray and marched off toward the garbage and recycling station.

"What's up with her?" asked Finch.

Samantha explained that she was transferring to another school for sixth grade. And she'd try to stay friends with Quinn, but it would be different. They'd be weekend friends.

Quinn was going to need a new school best friend.

"I'll ask her to do Green Team," promised Finch. "And Paleo Pals, too."

"That's pretty cool you started your own club," said Samantha.

"Thanks," said Finch, wondering, was Quinn the one? Would your best friend moving away be a good enough reason to write *Help* on a piece of paper and bury it in the school garden?

Samantha added, "And that you're, you know . . ."

"What?"

"You know, trying to do nice stuff for everybody."

"Thanks," he said again.

He took a swig of milk and stuck a fish stick in his mouth, pretending he wanted to eat so he wouldn't have to talk anymore. He wasn't sure why, but Samantha thanking him, which was really nice of her and should have made him feel really good, just made him feel really bad.

It wasn't that she knew the secret. It was that suddenly, he doubted inviting Quinn to be on Green Team or Paleo Pals was going to help much. Suddenly, he doubted he was helping anybody.

And so many kids needed help! There were sixteen kids in Mrs. Adler's class, not counting him. And all you had to do was a little digging to discover that almost all of them had some kind of problem.

He took another gulp and looked around at the hundred-and-fifty-odd kids munching fish sticks and carrot sticks. He felt himself rocking side to side, thinking. He was think-rocking. And rock-thinking. Probably every kid in this cafetorium had a problem. Probably every kid in Acorn Comprehensive had a problem. Probably—whoa. Too much rock-thinking. The milk he had swallowed was sloshing around inside him. It made his stomach hurt.

Finch stopped rocking, and his stomach felt a tiny bit better.

But now his head hurt. Because thinking about how every kid in school probably had a problem was just plain too big of a thought. It made his head feel so big and heavy that he set down his carton of milk, pushed his tray aside, and lowered his head onto the table. It touched down with a little thump.

Which felt . . . *good*, in a weird way. Thumping his head felt so . . . *thumpy*, that for a second it stopped all those other thoughts.

He did it again—*thump*—and kept his head down on the table.

"Finch, you okay?" asked Samantha.

Finch looked up but that was a mistake. All he had to do was look around to start thinking again about how he would never figure out who wrote the note. Better make it stop again. He lowered his head back down. *Thump.*

143

And how he wasn't helping anybody anyway. *Thump.*

And now he wasn't even going to Dinosaur State Park. *Thump.*

Because there was no way he was going to get all his work done by Friday! *Thump. Thump thump thump thump thump.*

"Finch, quit it!"

That sounded like Noah. Finch stopped thumping and picked up his head. It *was* Noah. And he wasn't alone.

Noasaurus

When Finch stopped thumping and picked up his head, there was Noah. No surprise. Also Samantha, still sitting across from him, and Quinn, back in her seat. Angelika was standing there, too. And so was David.

And so was Mr. White. Otherwise known as *Awesomeraptor.* "Finch!" he said. "What's up?"

Sometimes Finch thought up captions for the illustrated story of his life as a famous paleontologist. Sometimes he pretended he was a dinosaur. And sometimes, like right now, he mixed it up.

When Awesomeraptor *and* Finchosaurus *meet, the valley shakes with the force of their steps. They are two fierce predators. Will they fight?*

David spoke up. "Dino demo," he said.

"Dino demo?" asked Mr. White.

Awesomeraptor *is distracted by another dinosaur, who could be easier prey. He follows it down the valley.*

"Dinosaur demonstration," explained David. "He was

showing us how some dinosaurs have such a hard skull, they could pound it like crazy."

"*Pachycephalosaurus*," added Noah. "Its skull was, like, ten inches thick. We learned that in Paleo Pals."

Mr. White did not say *Awesome*, like usual.

Awesomeraptor *circles back to where he left* Finchosaurus.

"Finch," said Mr. White. "It's almost time for recess. Let's go to my office where we can talk."

Suddenly a Tyrannosaurus rex *comes between* Awesomeraptor *and* Finchosaurus.

"No!" said Angelika.

It's another deadly predator!

"She means—he can't," said Noah.

What sort of dinosaur should Noah be? wondered Finch. *Noasaurus*, of course! A small dinosaur from the late Cretaceous.

Noasaurus *walks slowly down the valley, looking like easy prey, drawing* Awesomeraptor *away from* Finchosaurus.

"Because he has to report to Mrs. Adler's room for recess," said Noah.

"So he can try to finish all his missing assignments," explained David.

"So he can go on the class trip," added Quinn.

"The end-of-the-year trip," echoed Samantha. "To Dinosaur State Park!"

Together, a pack of smaller dinosaurs is almost a match for a big predator.

Mr. White had a puzzled look on his face. He stood, tapping his finger to his white beard, as if he was trying to decide whether to turn "Let's go to my office" into a command. Or whether to back off.

"We're really, really sorry we disrupted lunch," said Samantha. "Really."

"And it won't ever, ever happen again," said David.

"Exactly what won't happen again?" asked Mr. White.

"No more *Pachycephalosaurus* demonstrations on the lunch tables," said Angelika.

"Promise," said Noah. "I'll sit with him every day and make sure."

Mr. White turned to Finch.

"You've been awfully quiet," he said. "Is there anything you want to say?"

There were a lot of things Finch wanted to know, but that he didn't want to say. Like, *Why is everybody being so nice to me?* Instead, he said the words that would make Mr. White go away.

"I won't bang my head on the table anymore," he said. "Promise."

"All right, then," agreed Mr. White. "And good luck finishing your work, Finch. I really hope you can go on the trip. I'm tagging along as chaperone, so I hope to see you then."

The bell rang just as Mr. White was walking away, and everyone scrambled to bus their lunch trays and head outside for recess. Everyone except Finch, Angelika, and Noah.

"That was awesome!" said Finch, laughing. "You guys were great!"

"That was not awesome," said Angelika. "You almost got in a lot of trouble!"

"That was not funny!" added Noah.

Whoa. That was strange. Noah thinking something *wasn't* funny?

"What?" cried Finch. "It was totally funny!"

"No," said Noah, shaking his head. "Not funny! I told you, I'm not going without you. So you better sit with me tomorrow, like I told Mr. White. I'm not kidding!"

The next day, Finch found out exactly how *not* kidding Noah was.

Noah stuck with Finch from Mrs. Adler's room to the cafetorium. He stuck with Finch in the lunch line. He stuck with Finch as they found a table and sat down.

Outside, rain was slooshing down the big cafetorium windows. Inside, the smell of chicken tacos filled the air. Finch opened his milk carton and stuck in his straw, as Angelika plunked her tray down beside Noah, and Fatouma plunked hers down beside Finch.

"Twelve times one," said Fatouma. "Go."

"What?" cried Finch.

"Fatouma's going to quiz you," said Noah.

"This is one of the things on your list, right?" asked Angelika. "What you need to finish so you can go on the class trip?"

"You asked me to help Millie with her times tables," said Fatouma. "And I did, and she passed. I can help you, too. Come on, twelve times one."

Instead of answering, Finch took a big bite of his chicken taco. This was so embarrassing! He didn't want anybody's help.

"Come on, Finch," pressed Noah. "This isn't all about you. What about me?"

Suddenly Finch felt like all that thumping yesterday had jiggled something loose in his brain. Good question. *What about Noah?* Noah's dog Rozzy was so old and sick she had to be carried outside so she could go to the bathroom, and that didn't just start happening last week. It could have been happening back when Finch found the note. How come he had been so quick to assume the note-writer wasn't Noah, just because Noah was helping him? He could have been faking!

"Here's the deal," he said. "I answer Fatouma's questions. You answer mine."

"Deal," said Noah, nodding.

"Twelve times one," said Fatouma.

149

"Twelve," answered Finch.

"No," said Fatouma, shaking her head. "Say the whole thing. Twelve times one is twelve. It works better that way."

"Twelve times one is twelve," said Finch, and turned to Noah. "Noah, was it you? Did you write the note?"

"What note?" asked Fatouma.

Fatouma already knew he was trying to help kids. She just hadn't known exactly *why*. But finding out the truth about Noah was more important than trying to keep a secret. Besides, it wasn't much of a secret anymore.

"I found a note," he explained. "Somebody wrote a note, asking for help."

"That's why you asked me to help Millie?" asked Fatouma.

"Yeah, basically," he answered. "I knew she needed help, and I thought you could help her, maybe. But I don't know if Millie wrote the note, or not. We still haven't figured out who wrote it." He turned back to Noah and asked again, "Was it you?"

"No," said Noah. "I mean, it stinks. You know. But it wasn't me. I swear."

"What stinks?" asked Angelika.

"His dog," said Finch.

"Your dog smells?" she asked Noah.

"Actually, yeah, she does a little," said Noah with a small smile. "But that's not it. She's really old, and the vet says it's time to . . . put her to sleep."

"Wow," said Angelika, giving Noah a sorry-for-him smile. "That's really sad."

For a second nobody said anything else. The cafetorium was filled with the buzz of kids all around them, talking, and the sound of the rain slooshing down the windows.

Finally, Fatouma broke their silence. "Twelve times two."

"Twelve times two is twenty-four," answered Finch, turning to Angelika. "What about you?"

"No," said Angelika. "I swear."

Finch turned to Fatouma.

"It wasn't me," said Fatouma. "But I'm kind of glad you found it."

"Why?"

Fatouma shrugged. "If you hadn't, you wouldn't have asked me to help Millie. And if you hadn't asked me, we wouldn't be friends now."

"Or be on Green Team," added Finch. "Don't forget Green Team. You better not quit next year just because you'll be in sixth grade."

"I won't," she said, grinning.

"All right, people," said Noah in his best Mrs. Adler imitation. "More math."

Everybody laughed and Fatouma went on to twelve times three.

By the end of the week, Finch and the number twelve were solid, and he knew a trick in case he forgot: break twelve into ten and two. For example, twelve times seven was the same thing as ten times seven plus two times seven, which was easy. That was seventy plus fourteen, which was eighty-four.

Finch had answers for his twelve-times test, but that still left him with one big question scratching at his brain. *Who? Who? Who?*

Iffosaurus

On the last day of the second-to-last week of school, Finch sat down on his bouncy chair and began to bob softly up and down. He looked at the clock: 8:30. In about five minutes, everyone was going to find out he hadn't tried his best.

Mrs. Adler went to the front of the room and raised her hand in the air, signaling for silence. Grammy Mary sat quietly with her hands in her lap, to model "paying attention." One by one, kids stopped talking.

Iffosaurus *appears on the scene, and a hush settles over the valley.*

"Listen up, fifth graders," said Mrs. Adler. "If you have handed in all your assignments, you will be cleaning out your desks this morning. We have an extra trash can, but please do not pick up the contents of your entire desk and toss everything into the trash. The green bin is for paper, and we are still recycling. I, for one, would love to end the year with a Golden Bucket Award. Wouldn't that be nice, Grammy Mary?"

"That would be awfully nice, Mrs. Adler," agreed Grammy Mary.

Mrs. Adler wrapped up her instructions. "For those of you who have not handed in all of your assignments, I will be meeting with you individually." Then she headed toward her desk in the back of the room.

Iffosaurus *walks slowly down the valley, and slowly, the smaller dinosaurs return to their foraging. For the moment, all seems safe. But suddenly,* Iffosaurus *stops.* Finchosaurus *holds still. If* Iffosaurus *is hungry, and she sees him, there is little he can do against this giant foe.*

"Finch," said Mrs. Adler. "Come here, please."

Finch followed Mrs. Adler. Standing by her desk, swaying back and forth, he had a funny feeling, as if people were watching. He snuck a peek. Noah was definitely watching and listening. Angelika, too. Other kids seemed to be cleaning their desks in slow motion. Quietly.

Mrs. Adler picked up a paper. "This is your *You Were There in Colonial Connecticut* essay. I have to say, I was very surprised."

Facing Iffosaurus, Finchosaurus *must decide—does he run? Or does he stay and fight?*

"Pleasantly surprised," added Mrs. Adler, as she handed Finch his essay, which had a giant smiley face in the upper right-hand corner. "This is wonderful, Finch! You've really captured how it felt to be a boy two hundred years ago, eating pancakes. It's imaginative and well written. Well done."

Finch was swaying back and forth, and so were his feelings. First he felt happy, because who doesn't like a smiley face on their homework? Then he felt hopeful, because maybe he'd get to go on the trip? Then he told himself he shouldn't get his hopes up because this was only one of the assignments. Besides, how could he take credit for something that wasn't his idea? He couldn't.

"Uh, thanks," he said. "But I kind of got the idea from Grammy Mary."

"She told me about your conversation," said Mrs. Adler, nodding. "That's fine. You were the one who used your resources and turned that material into something new."

"Really?" asked Finch.

"Really," said Mrs. Adler with a smile. "Now, are you ready for your multiplication test?"

"Uh . . . sure," said Finch.

He recited the twelve-times table. He raced through twelve times six. He remembered twelve times seven. He got eight—the even numbers were easier—but then he tripped up on twelve times nine. So he did Fatouma's trick. Twelve times nine was the same as ten times nine plus two times nine. That was ninety plus eighteen. That was 108. Then he cruised through to the end.

"Twelve times ten is 120," he said. "Twelve times eleven is 132, twelve times twelve is 144."

"Excellent!" said Mrs. Adler, and a few kids started clapping.

"Fifth graders," scolded Mrs. Adler, "we are cleaning our desks and minding our own business." But she didn't sound mad. She actually sounded happy. "Now, if you can hand in your acrostic poem, you'll be all set."

"I don't have it," said Finch.

The smile on Mrs. Adler's face sank into a frown. "Really? But I spoke with your mother and she said you had written one."

"No," he said. "Not really."

That wasn't exactly true. He *had* written a poem. But it wasn't a real poem. It was a joke. And he hadn't even finished.

Fidgeter
Impish
Nincompoop
Chicken
H

H he'd left blank, because what he really wanted it to be wasn't true. H for *Helper*.

Mrs. Adler drew a deep breath and put the this-hurts-me-more-than-it-hurts-you look on her face. "I am really disappointed, Finch," she said. "You know what this means, don't you?"

Finch nodded. Of course he knew what it meant! It meant he was a fidgeting, impish, nincompoopy chicken who wasn't going to Dinosaur State Park. It meant that she and Mr. White and his mom and his dad would all say they were "disappointed in him," which just meant that they would *pretend* to be sad and surprised that he had messed up.

Worst of all, it meant that Noah would be bummed. Not "disappointed"-bummed. Actually, seriously bummed for real, because he was Finch's friend. His best friend. Who actually cared.

"Mrs. Adler! Mrs. Adler!" called Noah, waving his hand back and forth.

"Noah, I'm extremely busy," said Mrs. Adler. "What is it?"

"Does he have until the end of the day?"

"Noah, this is really not your concern. But the answer is yes. If Finch makes up his mind to try, there is still time to hand in his poem. And I really hope he does," she added, in a voice that did not sound hopeful.

Back at his desk, Finch bobbed lightly up and down on his bouncy chair. He pulled a bunch of stuff from his desk, so he could pretend to be cleaning.

It seemed like all he did anymore was pretend.

He pretended he was a dinosaur. He pretended he was going to be a paleontologist. He pretended he was doing his best work.

The dinosaur pretending was like make-believe. In

make-believe, you knew what was real and what wasn't. He knew he wasn't really a dinosaur. Obviously. Maybe it was a little babyish, but it wasn't doing anything bad.

Pretending that he was going to be a paleontologist was another kind of make-believe. He really did want to be a paleontologist. It was like making a wish. Maybe it was stupid, because to be an actual scientist you probably had to go to a lot of school, and school was not something he was good at. But at least it wasn't wrong to wish something.

But pretending to other people that he had been doing his best—that was like telling a lie. He had told himself it was okay, but it wasn't. He could tell that from Noah's face, which looked scrunched up tight, the way it had when Noah was telling him about Rozzy being sick.

And now, pretending that he didn't care about the trip to Dinosaur State Park—that was ridiculous. He wasn't fooling anybody. Everybody knew how much he wanted to go.

Finch didn't like this feeling. He needed to feel something different. He bounced a little higher on his chair.

"Finch," said Mrs. Adler. "Settle down, please."

Finch didn't want to settle down. He wanted to bounce. Bounce, bounce, bounce.

"Finch!" said Mrs. Adler.

Bounce, bounce, bounce. Bounce bounce bounce bounce bounce!

"Finch! If you can't settle down, I will—"

Nobody heard what Mrs. Adler would do if Finch couldn't settle down, because everybody was laughing. Because Finch had bounced himself right off his chair and slam-landed on the floor. Which landed him out in the hallway with Grammy Mary so he could "collect himself."

Excellent. Out here he didn't have to see Noah, looking so bummed, which just made him feel more bummed than he already was. He was dreading lunch, when Noah would probably bite off his head.

The Day Was Dark as Night

Finch got his lunch of spaghetti and meatballs and made his way through the cafetorium. He plunked his tray down on the table where he and Noah always sat and slid onto the bench seat. David and Atticus were already there. But not Noah.

Finch scanned the room. There was Noah, wandering around like he was searching for a place to sit. Was Noah that mad? Was he ditching him? Noah never sat down, though. He just went from table to table, talking to different kids for a little bit and then moving on. Finally, he landed at their table.

Finch dug his spork into a meatball. "What took you so long?"

"No fair!" said Noah. "You got four meatballs and I only got three. I want one of yours!"

"But that's not fair, either," pointed out Atticus.

"Hey, whose side are you on?" joked Noah.

"Uh . . . Finch's?" said Atticus.

"And this is a bully-free zone," said David, grinning. "No stealing meatballs."

"Yeah," agreed Finch. "No bullying."

"Okay, okay," said Noah. "I'm just goofing around. But you kind of owe me."

Finch twirled up a sporkful of spaghetti. "Why?" he asked. "What for?"

"For helping you write your acrostic poem," said Noah as he pulled a pencil stub from his pocket. "Come on, let's do this."

"Noah," groaned Finch. "Give it up. It's over. I'm not going."

"Your name has five letters," argued Noah. "That's five words. You don't even have to think them up. We'll give you ideas and you can choose one."

"What if I don't want your help?"

"Then you would be totally two-faced," accused Noah. "You want to do all the helping but you won't take any help yourself."

David and Atticus were just listening now. They weren't saying anything anymore. It felt like they weren't even there. It was just him and Noah.

But what if Noah wasn't there, either? For a second, he imagined he was *Finchosaurus*, walking across a deserted plain.

The day was dark as night. A meteorite had crashed, and

dust covered the sun. All the other dinosaurs had died. Finchosaurus, *alone, would survive.*

Finch didn't like this feeling. He didn't want to be the only dinosaur left on the planet. He put down his spork and took the pencil and wrote a big letter F on a paper napkin. "Okay," he said. "Now what?"

"Duh," said David.

"Duh," echoed Atticus.

"Friend," they said in unison.

Finch looked at David with his mop of I'm-taller-than-you-think camouflage hair and sandy, shaggy-haired Atticus. He hardly knew them at the beginning of the year, but they were friends now. He added "riend" after the letter F to make Friend.

"Thanks, guys," he said.

Some kids were coming toward their table. Mohamed, Kael, and Khalid. They always sat together at lunch now, drawing comics.

"Hey, Finch," said Mohamed. He had the latest *Captain Underpants* book tucked under his arm. "Thanks for asking your mom to get more books."

"No problem," said Finch. "But, you know, it wasn't that big of a deal. Anybody can ask her."

"It was still nice of you," said Mohamed, shrugging.

"What do you have for us?" asked Noah.

"Cool," said Kael.

"Courageous," said Khalid.

"Caring," said Mohamed.

"Excellent," said Noah. "Thanks, guys."

Mohamed, Kael, and Khalid headed back to their table.

"That's what you were doing before?" asked Finch. "Asking kids for words?"

"You're welcome," said Noah, nodding. "Now write those down."

Finch was writing down words beginning with the letter C, when up came Charlotte, Haley, and Graciela.

"Angelika told us why she showed us that book," said Graciela. "*The Big Book of*—you know. 'Cause you guys are on, like, a mission?"

"So, that book was actually pretty good," said Charlotte. "It had this whole chapter on how to get rid of—you know—and how to not get them again."

Finch noticed the three girls all had their hair braided like Samantha and Quinn, in those spiky-ridged dinosaur braids.

"So, we think your 'I' word should be 'Insect-buster,'" said Haley.

"Insect-buster?" asked Noah. "What else do you have?"

"Umm, intelligent?" suggested Charlotte.

"Interesting?" tried Graciela.

"Okay, thanks a lot," said Noah.

The girls wished him luck and took off. Finch was still writing down all their I-word ideas when Atticus hissed,

"Bully alert!"

Oscar and Oliver were heading straight toward them. But when they reached the table they only stopped long enough to drop a napkin on Finch's tray, and then kept on walking.

Finch picked up the napkin and read aloud: "Not -a-tattletale."

"That's it?" demanded Noah. "I gave them the letter N and they come up with one word that's not even a real word?"

"Yeah, but I like it," said Finch. "It's funny."

"How'd you get them to go along?" asked David.

Noah explained. "I may have said something about Finch's brother, Sam. His big brother. His big, strong brother."

"You said Finch's brother would beat them up?" asked Atticus. "But that's threatening. That's like bullying, too!"

"I know," said Noah with a shrug. "But I'm trying to write a poem in ten minutes. I was desperate."

Atticus and David laughed, and so did Finch. He felt good. He had words for four out of the five letters of his name, scrawled on napkins.

All around them, kids were starting to bus their trays. In a minute, everyone here would go out to recess, except him. He had to spend recess in Mrs. Adler's room. But that was cool—he was going to copy out his poem and come up with his last word.

Then he spotted Mr. White's white hair and beard and

his green-and-white-checked shirt, all the way across the cafetorium. And Finch could feel it: *Awesomeraptor* was here for him.

A minute later he reached their table.

"Hi, guys!"

"Hi," echoed Finch, Noah, David, and Atticus.

"I'm glad I found you, Finch. I'd like to have a little chat with you about something. Let's go to my office."

"But—"

"No worries!" said Mr. White. "I already spoke with Mrs. Adler. She knows you'll be with me. You won't be in trouble. Come on."

Finch rose and picked up his tray, trying to think of a way out of another friendly chat with the social worker. But he couldn't think. The cafetorium was crazy-noisy and he was in the middle of a stampede toward the trash and tray drop-off place.

There were bins for all the different kinds of trash. The one for food waste had a picture of apple cores and banana peels. Another bin had a sign they'd made in Green Team, with a picture of milk cartons and the words *Recycling Saves Trees*. Finch tossed his paper trash in the recycling bin, pushed his tray through the little window to where the lunch ladies worked, and followed Mr. White to his office.

Rising Sixth Graders

"Have a seat," said Mr. White, pointing to a new chair.

"Nice!" said Finch, sitting down in a chair just like Mr. White's, except smaller. It could go up and down. It could swivel. It could rock back and forth.

Mr. White smiled. "I thought you'd like it. I ordered that after one of our talks, actually."

For the next few minutes, while Finch swiveled, and rocked back and forth, and went up and down, Mr. White talked. He wanted to let Finch know there was a chance he might not be back in the fall. It depended on whether Mrs. Blake came back to work or took more time off to be home with her baby. It hadn't been decided. But just in case he wasn't here next year, he wanted Finch to know how much he'd enjoyed getting to know him.

"What about Paleo Pals?" asked Finch.

"If I'm not here, I'm sure you can find another adviser. I'll put the word out, if needed." Mr. White tapped the watch on his wrist. "Maybe you should head to your room."

I'll see you on the class trip, I hope?"

The trip. The poem. *He hadn't written down his poem yet!*

Finch jumped up from the special chair and raced to Mrs. Adler's room.

"Hello, Finch!" said Grammy Mary with a smile.

Finch was out of breath from running. "Hey, Grammy Mary," he said, panting. "Hey, Mrs. Adler, can I still give you my poem?"

Before she could answer, the bell rang, and suddenly kids were filing quietly into the room and taking their seats. Grammy Mary smiled at everyone the way she always did, but Mrs. Adler had a surprised look on her face. She had been asking kids to do this all year, but it had never happened.

"Grammy Mary," she said. "Do you hear what I hear? I think I hear the sound of rising sixth graders!"

"I do, too!" said Grammy Mary.

Mrs. Adler turned back to Finch. "All right, Finch," she said. "What were you saying? You have your poem?"

"Kind of," he said. "But it's my sloppy copy. I need to copy it out, okay?"

"I'm happy to hear it," said Mrs. Adler. "Go right ahead."

Finch stuck his hand in his pocket but there was nothing in there except the Band-Aid box. And suddenly he remembered. The recycling bin in the cafetorium. He had thrown the napkins away.

"Umm, actually, I don't have it," he said. "I guess I lost it."

"You had it, but you lost it?" asked Mrs. Adler. She sighed a tired, end-of-the-year sigh. "Well, do you think you can remember it?"

"Mrs. Adler!" called Noah, waving his hand in the air. "Mrs. Adler! Mrs. Adler!"

"Yes, Noah?"

"So, I know this is kind of weird, but can Finch say his poem out loud? You know, recite it?"

Mrs. Adler sighed another tired sigh. The messy bun her hair was always pulled into looked even messier than usual. "I would love to hear Finch's poem," she said, "but an acrostic poem is a visual poem, so I also need to *see* it. Finch, do you want to write it on the whiteboard as you recite it?"

What was Noah doing? Finch had nothing. Nothing in his pocket. And nothing in his brain. He gaped at Noah. *What are you doing?*

Noah just gave him a look that said, *We got this.*

Finch walked slowly to the whiteboard. He picked up a marker. Holding his breath, he wrote a capital F.

Nothing.

Then David—the kid who Finch had donated his allowance for—stood up, along with Atticus.

And Finch remembered their word. With a deep breath, he added *riend,* to make *Friend.*

Then underneath the F he wrote the next letter of his name, a capital I.

Up rose Charlotte and Haley and Graciela. They'd given him three words, but Finch could only remember the funny one that wasn't really a word. Except he could make it a kind of a word with a hyphen. *Insect-buster.*

Next Finch wrote an N, and Oscar and Oliver got out of their seats. He was going to need two hyphens for this word. *Not-a-tattletale,* he wrote.

Below the N he wrote the letter C. Up stood Kael and Khalid and Mohamed, who waved his *Captain Underpants* book in the air. Finch added *aring* after the C to make *Caring.*

He had come to the end of his name. The letter H. They hadn't gotten to that letter during lunch. He was going to have to come up with something by himself. Right now.

And now it felt like everybody was holding their breath. The room was so quiet he could hear sounds coming faintly from all over the school. Kids outside for gym, shouting, and kids in music class, singing, and someone click-clacking down the hallway.

Finch gripped the marker. One more letter. One more word.

Finally, Noah stood. Then Angelika. Then all the other kids who weren't standing up yet. Fatouma and Millie and Quinn and Samantha. They were all rooting for him to come up with the last word. They were trying to help him.

Because he had tried to help them.

Helper, wrote Finch.

Arms crossed, Mrs. Adler paced from one end of the room to the other, staring at the words on the whiteboard.

Friend
Insect-buster
Not-a-tattletale
Caring
Helper

Suddenly she seemed to realize that the whole class was standing up. "I want to see all my rising sixth graders *in their seats*," she said.

Everyone scrambled to sit.

"I'm not sure what to say," she said, pacing the length of the room again. "What do you think, Grammy Mary?"

Grammy Mary didn't answer in words. She gave a thumbs-up with one hand, and then the other. Two thumbs up.

"Grammy Mary has spoken," said Mrs. Adler. "And I agree. Finch, it appears you have written an acrostic poem and finished all your work. You can go on the class trip."

Every Piece of Paper Has Two Sides

On June 19, Finch wasn't making believe he was a dinosaur, or pretending he was a paleontologist. He didn't need to. He was in dinosaur heaven.

He was in Dinosaur State Park.

He stood inside the big dome, on the walkway that overlooked the dinosaur tracks. He was three feet away from where a dinosaur had walked!

The park guy, Ranger Sam, wore a pair of tiny wire-rimmed glasses and carried a pair of huge binoculars on a strap across his shoulder, like he wasn't about to miss seeing anything, close up or far away.

"In 1966," he said, "Edward McCarthy was bulldozing this area to make way for a new building. Lucky for us, he saw something unusual. Lucky for us, when he saw something unusual, he didn't ignore it. He didn't say, 'I don't know what that is, so I'm just going to keep on bulldozing.' He stopped. He asked questions. And because of him, we are able to see the tracks that dinosaurs made about two hundred million years ago. But what about the fossils of the dinosaurs themselves?"

Finch's hand shot up. "Nobody found them!"

"Correct," said Ranger Sam. "No fossils of the dinosaur remains were ever found. But there's a lot we can tell from fossil tracks. We think the dinosaur was a predator, about twenty feet tall. We can tell this dinosaur was walking, not running. Now, let's look over here . . ."

Ranger Sam moved along, and everybody followed, mostly. Finch kept looking down at the deep shape pressed into the rock. He wondered what Edward McCarthy, bulldozer driver, did after his discovery. Did he keep hoping, every time he was on a bulldozing job, that he would find something so amazing? And then he never did? And did he care that nobody ever found fossils of the bones?

"Finch, come along," said Mrs. Adler. "Time for lunch."

Outside at the picnic area, under the blue sky, it was Finch's favorite warm-but-not-too-hot temperature. Mrs. Adler and Mrs. Tomlinson passed out brown-paper lunch bags. Mr. White poured water into paper cups for everyone and Finch's mom handed them out. And Grammy Mary drifted from table to table, making sure kids had what they needed.

"That ranger guy was cool," said Angelika. "He knows so much about dinosaurs!"

"Finch knows just as much," said Noah, loyally.

"No, I don't!" said Finch.

"Pretty much!" said Angelika. "I know! You should tell him you're president of Paleo Pals!"

"No way!" said Finch.

"Yes!" said Noah. "And then he'll be, like, why don't you come be my special assistant?"

"Quit it, you guys," said Finch. But he didn't mind. Noah and Angelika could tease all they wanted. Because this was the best day of his life.

One: Last week, Noah and the whole class had saved his butt by helping him write his acrostic poem.

Two: This morning Mrs. Stuckey had announced that the final winner of the Golden Bucket Award was Mrs. Adler's room! And then she had wished a very. Happy. Birthday. To . . . Finch Martin!

Three: He was here. Now. And his mom was opening a big box.

"Happy Birthday, Finch," she said.

Everyone sang "Happy Birthday to You," and Finch got to pass out cupcakes. His mom had made vanilla with chocolate frosting, and chocolate with vanilla frosting. Finch made his way around the picnic area, from table to table, to where kids were sitting here and there on the grass.

"Cupcake? Cupcake, anyone?"

When he was done, part of him wanted to go back to the table where Noah and Angelika were sitting, so he could eat cupcakes with them and let them tease him about dinosaurs.

But part of him wanted to be by himself. This was the best day of his life. Except for one thing: He still didn't know who had written the note. He hadn't gotten to the bottom of the story, like Guppy said. He felt bad he hadn't talked to Guppy in so long. He wanted to call, but he'd been waiting. Hoping he would figure out the answer, first.

He found a spot on the grass and sprawled out. Overhead, a breeze was pushing the clouds across the blue sky. It was rippling the leaves on the trees, too, sending whirligigs spinning down. Kids began catching the whirligigs, peeling open their seed pods and sticking them to their noses.

"Acorn Comprehensive fifth graders!" called Mrs. Tomlinson. "We are starting to clean up. In fifteen minutes Ranger Sam is going to help us make plaster casts of the tracks, so, let's get ready!"

Noah ran by with a whirligig stuck to his nose. "Finch!" he called. "Look at me, I'm *Triceratops*! Come on!"

Usually Finch would be right there, running and pretending to be a horned dinosaur. But he didn't go anywhere. Maybe if he looked at the note one more time . . .

He stuck his hand in his pocket and pulled out the Band-Aid box. He pried open the lid and pulled out the scrap of paper. He had looked at it so many times that the paper was getting soft and fuzzy.

He was remembering something else Ranger Sam had said, about *how to see*. Edward McCarthy didn't only see what he expected to see—rocks to bulldoze. He saw what was actually there in front of him.

"One more thing, Acorn fifth graders!" called Mrs. Adler. "Dinosaur State Park recycles! So, sort your garbage and put the paper plates and paper bags in the proper bin. Let's be good guests!"

Something floated into Finch's brain, like the clouds floating across the sky. Paper. Recycling. *Every piece of paper has two sides.*

He turned the scrap of paper over.

No words; he already knew that. But he saw something else: The paper wasn't white. It was a faint, pale purple.

Purple?

Finch looked up. Looked around. Grammy Mary was sitting at one of the picnic tables with the other grown-ups. He went over and squeezed onto the bench seat between her and his mom. He put the note on the table.

"Grammy Mary," he said. "Did you write this?"

Grammy Mary smiled one of her big Grammy Mary smiles. But then she put her hands over her mouth, the way people did when they were . . . crying! And then tears were trickling down her cheeks.

"Mary!" said Mrs. Adler. "What is it? What's wrong?"

"Nothing's wrong," said Grammy Mary.

She picked up the scrap of paper, turning it over in her hands to show them: pale purple color on one side, and on the other side, the word *Help*.

"I always want all the kids to have a good day," she began. "But sometimes I feel I can't do very much."

"You always smile at everyone," said Finch.

"I know," she said, smiling. "But it doesn't feel like enough. So, one day, I said a little prayer. I wished that I could help each of you, just a little bit. I wrote down my prayer on my stationery. And later that day, when we were working in the garden planting lettuce seeds, I planted it."

"Let me guess," said Finch's mom. "Finch dug it up?"

Grammy Mary laughed her tinkling ice-cream-truck-song laugh. "He did indeed! I didn't know what to do, so I thought I would just wait and see. And, well, I don't mean to sound corny, but my prayer was answered in ways I never could have imagined!"

The grown-ups were strangely silent.

Mrs. Adler wasn't saying, "If you had . . ."

Mr. White wasn't saying, "Awesome!"

Finally, his mom asked, "Is this what you've been so busy doing the last few weeks? Trying to help other kids?"

Finch nodded. Yes.

"This is why you insisted I make sure the library owned every single copy of *Captain Underpants*?" she asked. "For Mohamed?"

Finch nodded again.

"And that's why Mohamed began bringing Kael and

Khalid to Mrs. Haywood's drawing time?" asked Mr. White. "Because he owed you a favor?"

Another nod.

"What about Millie's multiplication tables?" asked Mrs. Adler. "Did you have something to do with that?"

"I asked Fatouma if she would help her," explained Finch.

"What about *The Big Book of Parasites*?" asked his mom. "What was that all about?"

"That was Angelika," he said. "She figured out that Charlotte, Haley, and Graciela might need help with . . . uh, *that*. Noah helped, too," he added. But he didn't add exactly *how* Noah had helped—by figuring out that David was getting shaken down for lunch money. Because he still didn't want to tell on Oscar and Oliver.

"And does this have something to do with your unusual poem recitation?" asked Mrs. Adler. "The kids all standing up for you, because you had helped everyone?"

"I guess," said Finch. "Except I didn't. Not really."

"Look around you," said Grammy Mary, sweeping her hand through the air. "I think you've done more than you know."

Finch scanned the picnic area. He saw Atticus and David eating cupcakes side by side. Fatouma and Millie playing a clapping game. Mohamed and Kael and Khalid sitting in a triangle on the grass, laughing about something. Angelika and Noah and everyone else goofing off like they were kindergartners again, running around with whirligig

seed pods stuck to their noses.

Maybe Grammy Mary was right. If things had gone the way he wanted, it would have been just him helping just one kid. Instead, every time he had let someone in on the secret, they had turned into a helper-kid. By the end, who was a helper and who was getting helped was all mixed up.

It wasn't what he had planned. It was better.

Grammy Mary seemed to read his thoughts. "I think the seed I planted grew into something extraordinary," she said.

"Well, I think it's awesome," said Mr. White. "And I ought to know, since I'm . . . *Awesomeraptor!*"

"You know about that?" cried Finch.

Grinning, Mr. White nodded. "I know a little bit," he said. "I knew what you called me—and I knew something was going on. I just didn't know the whole story."

"It's quite a story," said his mom, giving him a hug. "Maybe it will be a book someday."

"Mom, don't go all librarian on me," said Finch.

But he was imagining this picture, like a page in a book. Blue sky. Trees with green leaves. Kids running around with whirligigs on their noses, pretending to be horned dinosaurs. Kids with new friends. What would the caption to this picture be? *Atticus Finch Martin, discoverer of the* Finchosaurus, *the largest dinosaur ever to roam the earth . . .*

He didn't know the rest. But it was going to be good.

About the Author

Gail Donovan is the author of the middle-grade novels *The Waffler, What's Bugging Bailey Blecker?*, and *In Memory of Gorfman T. Frog*, which was named a New York Public Library Best Books for Children. She is also an author for the Rainbow Fish & Friends picture book series based on the bestselling books of Marcus Pfister. Donovan, who was born and raised in Connecticut, lives in Maine with her husband and two daughters, where, in addition to writing children's books, she is a library assistant at the Portland Public Library.